Dark Paralysis

Craig P. Wilson

K-Oz Publishing

I humbly offer this story to those that dwell in the darkness.

Between the light and the darkness, there exists a realm without boundaries; it's here that the Shadows move on their own.
CRAIG P. WILSON

Contents

Preface

Sleep Paralysis is a widespread condition that is believed to occur in one's life at least once with 7.6 percent of the population. The first clinical documentation of Dark Paralysis was published in 1664 by a Dutch Physician. The doctor termed the condition as a nightmare or an incubus. Sleep Paralysis occurs during REM sleep when one dreams. The brain shuts the body's muscles down during REM sleep to prevent one from injuring themselves. The Paralysis occurs when one becomes aware while in this state and cannot move; this is the basic science, so they say. I suffered from Sleep Paralysis once. My experience was far more macabre than not being able to move. I was in my twenties and had been up partying for a few days. I'd drifted asleep in bed while watching TV; I was on my back. I remember feeling a burning current in my legs, and just as I tried to wake up, I felt a tremendous weight on my chest. My first instinct was to move my arms; I remember feeling as though they were being held down, as well as my legs. At this moment, I truly felt a foreign presence in the room, and there was more than one. I could feel that whatever was constricting me meant me harm. I never opened my eyes as I was struggling to breathe. The attack seemed to go on for minutes as my anxiety grew, making it harder to get oxygen to my cells. Eventually, I was able to move my small toe, which led to moving my foot; soon, I was sitting up enjoying deep breaths of air. I immediately started accusing my partner of trying to smother me. She'd been wrapping presents in the closet and had not been paying attention to me. Soon she'd become irritated with my questions, and I knew she'd had no idea of what I was talking about. This human had told me that I'd been talking to her just a few minutes prior; the timeline seemed much shorter than the experience of the attack.Although I never opened my eyes, I could feel others around me. I did not feel as though I was in my room, of which the lights were on the entire time. Those that do open their eyes have spoken of intruders such as Shadowmen, Aliens, demons, cats, and witches. Scientists term these visitors as hallucinations; I do not. These same researchers would have you believe that one cannot be harmed during the Dark Paralysis. Who's to say that SADS or Sudden Arrhythmic Death Syndrome isn't linked to the Paralysis? My heart was racing as I struggled to breathe, but what if I'd seen those who'd I'd felt holding me down? I believe that science may explain how one might transport to the Shadowland, but once there, that human is in a supernatural realm. Not knowing about Dark Paralysis is the best way of not thinking about it. For those of you that will search deeper, try not to sleep on your back.

Chapter 1

A very Long time ago....

As though in a trance, Billy Jones watches his Carnival Brethren work like ants, each methodically fulfilling their responsibilities. Although Bill is only 25 years old, he's considered a full Carney, with over 22 years of experience. Watching the transformation of superficial dirt and grass form into an oasis of lights, pleasures, and tastes still deeply moves this thoughtful man. Bill's in charge of the marble toss. A simple game that requires the contestant to throw and land a marble onto a large deep-lipped plate that unknown to the contestant is heavily greased. Every once and a while, a fortunate player will select the right dish that's less slick. With some average skill, the player will toss the marble in the right spot, winning one of the large, uniquely stuffed animals. The Never Sleep Swing Company or N.S.S.C Amusements had taken Bill into its embrace when his Mother abandoned him with the Carnival on his third birthday. He wasn't the first child to be dumped on the gypsy camp. Bill was born with many issues with his health. One leg was considerably shorter than the other. His eyes were too far apart and different colors, one a bright blue, the other a dark green; a massive brow crawls above in single file. Unknowing to him, it had been the curse of his stuttering speech that has pushed her over the edge. The owner of the N.C.C.S, The Count, a man who only sees potential in any form, had quickly placed young Bill with one of the Moms. These are members of the Carnival that give an unwanted child the love that would help develop youth into a valued member of the company. Over time, Bill's stutter began to fade. In moments of nervousness, his jousting tongue still slithers, but to his adopted family, his stutter is a forewarning of danger on the horizon.

The Count never hesitates to speak to his children of this matter, as he's lost Brethren over the years to the darkened alleys of unfriendly towns. For the past few days, Bill has felt the slithering wanting to strike as the horse-driven company had come closer and closer to the village of Greenbud. In this infamous place, there are many stills to keep the shine flowing. The company is on their leased dirt for the week; it's never a question of whether there would be trouble, but when? The Count doesn't like his children to leave the grounds, unless necessary, anywhere, but Greenbud is one of the places he forbids it. "They love to spend their money the night before, but once awake with severe headaches the next day. They can't stand that they've lost. It doesn't take much for the Jackals in this forsaken place to turn from the few morals they live by." The first time Bill had heard his leader give this speech, he'd felt the sincerity in his voice. Their impressive leader has broken down and cried while speaking of this subject. The breakdown occurs in towns like Greenbud, where he'd violently lost some of his beloved family. Unlike many owners in this dark underground lifestyle, The Count isn't just in it to make money; he'd been raised in high society with so much expectation. At a young age, he'd seen what greed could do to a man. The Count's Father had been a hoarder of success, only driven to serve his family. The practice of evil acts to achieve his own goals hardly needn't be justified within. With slicked long black hair, more than average height, and a medical degree, The Boss could have done anything with his life. Taking in the strays and turning them into good productive humans is his true passion. In Billy Jone's opinion, the speech The Count had made earlier in the night had been the best he'd ever felt from their leader. The buddy system had never formed quicker. Those in the camp would check on their co-workers each night or walk around each day, shadowing the potential trouble makers. It had been the speech that had put his flickering tongue to rest for the moment. Still, as the migrating rabbit hole so quickly forms in front of his eyes, Billy can't ignore the flapping Butterfly wings he can feel deep within his core.

As usual, the Carnival opens at dusk, and the long line of young and old humans begins to filter in. Many of these hearts are innocent, full of excitement and anticipation. Just as many are hardened with lower inhibitions while drunk on the shine, sipping that snake juice brings forth the demons who love to play. Bill momentarily loses touch with anxiety as he sees The Brother's bringing him a wooden cart full of new hand-sewn animals. Leonard, Joey, and Felix, what a wonderful sight they are. Joey and Felix are Dwarf twins; Leonard is a towering six-foot-seven giant. All three of them have blond hair and blue eyes, considered to be good-looking by most women. Other than Leonard's much more powerful stature, even the most dim-witted of these derelict locals couldn't mistake them for being Brothers. They move in their usual sequence, Joey always in the front, the mouth, the speaker of the house, and the unit leader. Felix is the brains of the three, who always tells it how it is. Not far behind is the muscle, pulling the cart with one hand and with the other, carrying his three-legged black cat named "Stitch." Leonard had been peeing in the woods when he'd come upon the black cat of which had been a bloodied mess; some-thing had torn its back leg off. The significant Carney rarely al-lows the cat out of sight since nursing it back to health.

"We have a lovely bunch of critters for yaw Billy." "I'll do my best not to adopt too many out this week, Joey." After their usual banter, the Carney sets up the handmade prizes. He stands on a stool advertising to all that walk by; it's a slow process initially. The first night is usually his worst, as he hasn't made any re-lationships with the townsfolk. Throughout the weekend, and some small prizes handed out for free, as well as bigger prizes, won, the money always rolls in.

"What's the charge for a toss, hoss?" Before answering, Bill instinctively inspects the small man in front of him; he's in his work clothes and is very dirty. Billy smells the whiskey that steams through the man's filthy pores as though he's marinated with it; his eyes are dark and small, suggesting a sure void of empathy. "A penny for a toss, ten for a nickel, my friend," "We're friends now, are we?" the foul specimen replies. Bill freezes; he feels his tongue convulsing. Rather than answer in a stutter, he just stares at the man.

"Cat got your tongue, young fellow," Billy can't take his eyes off the rotted teeth that putridly line his mouth. "I'd tend to think that because we're such good friends that I'd get a better rate, boy." "I'll give you fifteen tosses for a nickel," Bill manages. "Sold," the drunkard shouts before taking a small bottle out of his filthy coat and gulping back a good swig. Carl Hester takes his time, pretending as though he's checking the wind while promoting his skills to other locals that are walking by; soon, a small crowd has surrounded them. It's easy for Bill to see this man is infamous in the rowdy town. Hester's checking out all of the plates, soon spotting a dull-looking one, feeling as though he's solved the puzzle. "I'll shoot for that one boy," Bill says nothing, as he knows this clown understands the hustle. Carl gently tosses his first marble as though he's been doing it his whole life. The attempt is just a little heavy, and the marble rolls off; the small crowd screams in disappointment. "Have faith, my friends; I've got it figured out," he promises before taking another swallow of his firewater. Bill feels the darkness coming; there's no doubt he's about to have a problem. Quickly he gives the nod to Mikey; the spotter directly goes to fetch The Brothers. Carl, loving the attention he's getting, playing to the small crowd, points to a little girl, "Your first honey, come on over." She hesitates a little shy; her mother assures her that everything is fine and that Mr. Hester is a good man. "If I sink this here, marble young lady, you get to pick the prize and keep it." The little girl smiles as the gathering crowd cheers on his generosity. After another gulp, Carl tosses the marble, and this time it sticks; the crowd cheers in triumph, as one of their own has beaten the odds! "Nice throw, sir," Bill compliments the winner. "Which one would you like, young lady," Carl asks, completely ignoring the

Carney. "I'd like that big bear over there, Mister." "You heard her, boy, she'll take that one, hurry up!" Bill quickly retrieves the handmade prize and hands it to the little girl; the soft bear is almost as big as her. "Do you see how easy it is folks, step right up, and give it a try; only two throws it took this...." "I ain't finished boy, seems to me we had a deal for fifteen tosses, and I only did two, so to my calculations, that leaves another thirteen." "I'm sorry, sir, but once you land one, the games up, it says it right there on the sign." Carl faces the crowd, "That little sign boy, can you see that, my Friends," the hero shouts! "Sure can't, Carl!" "He's trying to play you for a fool, Hester!" "Supposed I can't read, boy," Carl asks Bill? "That's no fault of mine Sir," The gamesman knows he'd made a mistake and should have explained this important rule; the wings within flap so hard he's ready to vomit. "Seems to me you should have explained this rule during our negotiations, boy." "That's right, Carl, you tell him," someone shouts from the crowd! Hester's pointing to a boy in the crowd, utterly oblivious to what Bill's trying to explain, The Brothers show up. How quickly the crowd quiets at the sight of the Dwarfs and the giant carrying the cat. "What's the problem here Bill," Joey asks? Before the gamer can answer, thankfully as his tongue is dancing, the local interrupts, "Your man here made a deal for fifteen throws. I nailed her on the second, and now he's telling me I'm out of throws shorty!" "That sign right up there states our policy on a winning throw...." "Maybe I don't read tiny!" A strong rumble of laughter comes from the crowd. "That wouldn't surprise me, Sir, and my very tall, strong partner here, Leonard, I'm sure would be more than happy to take you somewhere and give you some lessons," The crowd becomes still. Joey singles for the local to bend over and whispers, "Or we could give you a couple of free tickets to our gentleman's tent, Sir. You and some of your friends can check out the naked dancing later on." "And if I decide, I'd rather toss more marbles shorty?" "Then my large associate will be forced to toss you out. As popular as you seem to be with the locals, I'm sure they'll forget quickly and enjoy their freedom to come and go as they please for the rest of the week." Carl Hester can't stand to lose and hates to be wrong. He's also aware that getting tossed from the grounds will prevent him from all kinds of wicked fun over the next couple of days. "I guess I should have read the sign, my friends." As quickly as the local heartlessly mutters these words, a dark end game plays out in his mind. Felix grabs Joey's arm right before his twin Brother gives the tickets to the local; he gives him a look, the signal that they need to speak. "Excuse me for a moment, Sir," he follows his twin until they're out of hearing range. "We need to get rid of this guy Joey." "Billy should have explained the rules better; this yahoo has a point, Brother." "I'm getting an evil vibe off this snake; he's smart, real smart, and isn't going to drop it, Brother." Joey thinks about it for a minute; "It's not how The Count does business, Felix. Indirectly this was our fault; he has a valid point. We'll put a shadow on him, okay?" Felix just nods, suggesting he accepts the decision; but disagrees with it.

Once given the tickets, Carl immediately begins slithering around, searching for reinforcements to help grease the gears of private justice. He could have just gone to the drinking tent, where he would have undoubtedly run into many comrades, but as Felix stated, Carl's way too smart to show a good card hand. Over the next few hours, slowly sipping, Hester slithers through the bright lights and delicious smells, watching his town's people spending money and having fun. The fire burns within as he watches them, giving away their hard-earned dollars to what he views as a complete hustle and nothing more. Carl believes himself to be a good God-fearing man, a human of high morals and principles. By the time he's ready to use his free tickets, he's recruited three other men that he also considers to be God respecting folk. Aaron Rogers, John Hoble, and Whitey Finn have Hester's back and are down for anything. Carl only needs to spend a few casual minutes with each, explaining the situation and expectations before handing them a comp ticket for the tent.

His recruits are behind him all the way. The four men arrive early, spreading themselves throughout the entrance line. The hunters then strategically place themselves around the large tent; each has a good whiskey buzz and is quite ready to stir the pot. The Brothers amongst other fighting men are also in place, as they are every night in the gentleman's tent. This attraction is the most lucrative, but where the most potential for trouble lies. The Mud Duck band's introduced. The country swing kicks in full as the dancing beauties fill the stage, moving seductively with the pure intent of making money. The testosterone in the tent can be felt rising as the ale is served while hard-working cash changes hands. The girls target their marks and begin to reach out into the crowd. Carl wastes no time rushing the wooden stage, now doing his jig, as he plays to the group. The girls have no idea of this customer's argument with the company and begin to follow his lead; in no time, Carl pulls down one of the lady's tops, and the chaos ensues! After handing his cat to Felix, Leonard rushes to the stage; he's stopped by John Hoble, the giant of Carl's recruits before he can grab Hester. Hoble is as mean as he is enormous, and Hester is shocked as he watches the Carney put his friend down quickly with a few devastating punches to the head! Leonard's much more versed in the art of hand-to-hand relations than the large local. The ladies are escorted off the stage as multiple fights have broken out. Ears are bitten as fingers are broken; the final result is the tent being shut down! Quite a few of the local men are escorted from the leased land in a very unfriendly fashion as well. The police eventually arrive, and The Count sorts it all out with a small payoff to one of the deputies.

Much later in the night, The Count sits down with The Brothers; he's pretty upset but understands Joey's choice of letting the man stay on the property. "Billy knows better; he's been, nervous, boys. We'll move forward, and if things seem to be jaded, we'll cut our losses and move from this hole."

Another meeting takes place that night. As the whiskey is guzzled back by these local coyotes, the distribution of private justice is set in motion.

Early the following day, The Count calls a meeting; every Carney, from the strong man to the alligator boy, has heard what happened. Billy feels as though the inside of his mouth will bleed as his tongue batters every inch of it, as he manages to apologize to the entire camp. His Brethren soothes and forgives, knowing he's as good as any man that lives.

Over the next few days, the Carnival runs like a Swiss watch, the smooth exchange of currency for pure fun and entertainment. Security is the least busy division of the company. Their primary duties are tasks of help, whether it be directions to outhouses, lost children, or the many men who've overdrank and need a place to rest. Most of the locals are happy and speak well of The Never Sleep Swing Company. Still, under this candy-coated circus, the dark plan of the coyotes is slowly forming by way of four young women, who've been tasked to target The Brothers and Bill Jones. Elsie, Betsy, Irene, and Joyce start slow, smiling at first, and as the rides turn and the cotton candy is served, introductions are made. A gentle touch here and there, licks of the lips, and swings of the hips; until there's no doubt in the unsuspecting Carney's minds that these local girls want to make a party. Having relations with locals is nothing new for many old enough members of the Never Sleep Swing Company. Whether it's a side business or simply pleasure, it's a widely accepted practice, and this is why on the last night, The Brothers are convinced they're safe to leave the leased land with these girls. Led by a chance at easy romance, they ignore the constant warnings from Bill Jones. Once he knows they're going, he promises to keep his stuttering tongue to himself. Joey loves bigger girls, and this Irene is one of the sexiest, roundest creatures he's ever laid eyes on. He ignores the pleading of his longtime friend; "It doesn't seem right, Joey. They're being so adamant about us fellows following them, that, and I've seen them looking at one another with the devil in their eyes; these gals are wolves in a sheep's disguise." "Us Brothers are willing to take the risk. Billy, we talked about it last night and agreed these ladies are of a welcoming nature. If you don't want no free pleasure, that's fine; but don't go wrecking this for us." Once again, Bill promises to keep their wandering to himself, but as he watches them disappear around the fence and into the darkness, more than a foreboding feeling of dread washes over him. This good man only lasts twenty minutes after they leave before rushing to The Count's tent; he doesn't care how mad they are, as long as they're alive to be so.

As much as The Count wants to slap and scream at Billy, he doesn't, instinctively knowing that at this moment, time is all that matters. An extensive search party is assembled, each is armed with weapons ranging from knives to pitchforks, and around the path and into the darkness they go. The Count takes a few with him and goes to the sheriffs. He hopes the fringe benefits of free dances during the week and the nightly payment he's been giving the greedy local lawman will pay a dividend in this jaded moment. The grey-haired Sheriff has forgotten the gratuities he's been provided by the man who stands, unwelcomed in his home. "This ain't good partner! I've been telling you to keep your mutts on a chain all week, haven't I? This town has way more dark alleys than anyone's going to find with their eyes. If these girls come to me with accusations, making trouble, I'm going to tax you heavily." The Count knows this man is as crooked as an alligator's smile. During each corrupt exchange, a look of hate is never far from the surface of the lawman's face. Filled with dread, The Count follows the dirty officer deep into the dark forest; it's his love for the Brothers that fight against his instincts. Unknowing to The Count, Sheriff Dale Beachwood has already heard about the plans of Hester and his boys, and he has no plans of stepping in front of that rabid pack. When these gypsies move on out, he has to live with them, and Hester is very influential when it comes to who's voted in as Sheriff every four years.

The Brothers are cautious. They follow the human lures into the dark barn after the very long walk; the lanterns are lit, and the unsuspecting men begin to relax. The small group quickly becomes engaged in drinking and socializing. These fellows are well-traveled, cultured, and prove to be much better company than the local men these women are accustomed to. Over the next couple of hours, they get to know each other; two of these strangers become very intimate as they casually slip away. Three of the ladies are ready to tell the drunken game that they're being hunted. Elsie, Ilene, and Betsy read each other as they laugh at The Brother's jokes, looking at one another and the unsuspecting with eyes of empathy. Unlike their unspoken leader, Joyce, these three humans are good, but the life of John Hoble's wife has been one of loneliness and abuse. Her conditioned obedience keeps her on track. Joyce had listened to her husband yell and scream all night after the rough treatment he'd received in the gentleman's tent. As if it hadn't been bad enough that her big dummy had been staring at other women naked, she'd tended to his wounds; it had somehow become her fault in the end. This is why Joyce was more than happy to help out with Carl Hester's dark plan of private justice. As these dirty men drink the local moonshine, so naïve for such well-traveled big shots, she keeps a close watch on her fellow conspirers. Joyce warns them to keep their mouths shut, with her stoned cold glances; knowing, her so-called friends don't have the stomach for this type of wet work. As the second bottle of white lightning is almost finished, it's the sad story of how these boy's Mother had passed, beaten to death. The genuine tears in these men's eyes finally break Elsie's loyalty. She no longer cares how she'll be frowned upon or treated by those that will undoubtedly hear of her betrayal. "This isn't right, Joyce; I'm not going to be a part of this!" Joey quickly stands up, he's drunk, and it takes him a moment to find his footing; "It's alright dear, you don't have to do anything you don't want to; just show us back to...." "Shut your mouth, Elsie, cause you know what's going...." Felix cuts in; "Why have you brought us out here, Ladies?" Before the simple question can be answered, torches are seen shining through cracks in the walls, accompanied by the wicked drunken howling of the large circling pack! "I'm so sorry," the three good ladies mutter as their heads are to the ground, unable to look into the eyes of the men they've set up. The large quiet giant, hands Stitch to Felix. Leonard hasn't consumed much, as his internal compass has been pointing to the wrong. The energy of these local women is jaded. The giant grabs hold of Joyce; she pees herself as she's easily lifted. "Your neck's the first to be snapped if we don't get out of this fix, as the gods are my witnesses." Like a sack of potatoes, he carries her to the barn door; her kicking, screaming, and scratching have the effect of a fly on an elephant.

"We have your ladies in here, boys! This one, Joyce, the ugly one; I could break her neck like a twig!" Leonard gives her a good pinch on one of her thick love handles, producing a deafening scream! Some of the hunters come into view. Leonard puts one of his large hands over the mouth of the frantic lure and eases up the grip, for he has no intention of hurting her until this point; "Joey, Felix, get over here!" The twin Dwarfs stagger over, joining Leonard at the door; they both sober up as they take in the bizarre sight outside. The four men are all wearing dresses. Each wears a mask of overdramatized make-up, the lipstick reaching far past the edges of their lips. "We can find new lady's boys; it makes no difference to us." Hester's voice sounds like an aged granny's; Felix and Joey are paralyzed with fear, but Leonard's in full fight mode. "Come on in, you dirty copperheads!"

Felix suddenly feels heat from behind. The dwarf turns around, facing the dozens of torches held by the drunken crossed dressed, bloodthirsty mob; he whispers, "May the gods have mercy." Leonard charges the pack; the giant is as fierce as he is big. His initial rush would have given him escape if he'd wanted, as the fake rabid Tranny's split quickly, all shocked by the quickness and power of the massive man. He could've run straight through the back door, but this good man isn't about surviving; he'd never let harm come to his tiny kin. In that first moment, more than one of their make-up slathered jaws are broken; however, there are too many brave men in this pack, and soon a pitchfork goes into the giant's thigh. It still takes another minute for Leonard to drop to his knees, driving the sharp farm tool further into his flesh. Yet, he still grabs and punches, desperate to free his two Brothers from the agony he knows is coming!

"That's enough, ladies," Hester slithers, this new voice even foreign to the ones that have known him for years, causing some local hairs to rise as well. "What's the rush? These boys are as good as dead. They've been bad for a very long time, taking good people's money on the hustle. We're going to make an example of these snakes." "Listen, Sir, if you let us go, we'll leave it at this; no one will know any better. We'll lick our wounds and be out of town tomorrow." "Is that any way to address a lady," again with the creepy voice? Hester takes a long sip of moonshine, followed by a lick of the lips and a queer laugh. Joey and Felix both stare at the lipstick that's smudged around the mouth and the dirty, blackened stubbed teeth that Carl uses to chew his food with. This moment is of pure Macabre as the torches burn, dancing to heavy breathing upon the eerie silence lathered in sweat and liquor. "Don't beg that man, Joey; he's the head-copperhead, and the rest are just a gaggle of servants," Leonard screams! "Some of you gals start getting the tar heated outback..." the leader begins to instruct, just before Felix drops Stitch, and as hard as he can, kicks the freak square in the scrotum. Hester falls to the ground, shrieking in pain; the others grab the Dwarf quickly and begin beating him savagely! Joey drops himself into the cauldron of abuse and somehow manages to take his twin brother's hand! They're kicked, stomped, stabbed, and smashed; it isn't long before they are out cold and no longer aware!

Stitch sneaks through the chaos and rubs against Leonard, who's been tied up, and lies on his side. The pitchfork has been yanked out. One of the drunken trannies has slowed the leaking of blood by tying a rope around his tree-trunk thigh, assuring the giant's participation in the upcoming ritual is a must. Joyce sees the black cat; "Is this your baby, big fellow?" Leonard refuses to give satisfaction to these bastards by showing any emotions; the good man knows they've hit a dead-end. "I'll take care of your crippled pet; well, our special girls have a little killing time. Okay, big man?"

Hester's managed to get to his feet; his testicles have been damaged badly. "Hang all three over there; it's a perfect spot to tenderize them before feathering them!" Once hung in the corner, the strangest of parties ensues; a fiddle, guitar, and hand-drum are brought to the old barn and lots more moonshine. Men in drag take turns, punching, kicking, and slicing up the Carney's as the tar heats up. Three large satchels of chicken feathers are placed under their hanging feet. Every so often, they're splashed with water in the face to keep them conscious.

With each sip of the shine, the imaginations of these crossed-dressed psychopaths become more creative! Urination on The Brothers is followed by pig feces being wiped upon their open wounds. Some of these ravenous drunkards work in twos, one cuts, as the other strips a small piece of flesh; how powerful they all feel in this moment of chaos. As brutal and painful as each act of torture is, there's no threat of life loss, as inflicting pain is the primary goal of this savage ritual. Joyce sits front and center with Stitch in her lap; the cat stays still but just keeps on letting off a high-pitched call, only she can hear, as the music is quite loud. Leonard keeps a cold stare on her during the Dixie torture. The local girl can tell by the look in his eyes that if given a chance, he'd tear her apart with those massive hands. Over and over, she sticks her tongue out at him as if they're children playing a dangerous game behind the schoolhouse.

Hester's had to sit still; it feels as though something popped inside his scrotum. He's furious, as the ugly Dwarf has, in a way, taken this special privilege away from him. Carl suffers in silence, trying to catch his breath as the lynching unfolds. One of his cronies informs Hester the tar is ready, he readies himself to lead. Trying to hide the pain, the gross drag queen gimps over to The Brothers and pulls out a razor; he's used the blade to shave since he was sixteen. "Time to go to sleep, gentleman, time to run out your lights, boys," and as the creepy tone slithers from his mouth, Joyce carries Stitch to a large basin of dirty water. Leonard watches as his three-legged beauty kicks and scratches to survive and wonders in this moment of terror if they'll meet again on the other side? Will he finally sleep peacefully?

For a split second, just as the dark queen digs the old razor into the bruised flesh of Joey's throat, Leonard sees the Shadow of a black cat come to life on the wall of the barn. Slowly it glides over the weathered wooden panels until he can feel its presence as he hangs with his Brothers in the corner. Leonard feels the energy as though his skin is gently being caressed. He can no longer see the menacing Shadow of the cat, yet he knows Stitch is waiting to welcome him and his Brothers into the darkness. Leonard turns his attention to the loud gurgling of his Brothers as their blood runs from their throats; strangely enough, comfort comes over him, as he knows they'll feel no more pain. Leonards eye to eye with the ugly face of the man who'd only gone to the Carnival in hopes of finding a moment like this; "Should have let me finish tossing those marbles, I guess, eh big boy?" The voice is deep, angry, as though it's being funneled through a filter that's based on a life of abuse and disappointment, the older woman's voice gone, giving way to this demonic tone. As he feels the cold blade dig into his throat, Leonard smiles as he sees the giant Shadow of Stitch rise behind the evil that's just assured his expiration. Each of the Brother's spirits spikes at one more attempt of life as the hot tar is poured from above, searing their flesh, igniting their cells. The Shadow-cat watches as the dixie-drag-queens smother the tar with feathers. As the tar hardens, life completely slips from each of the gruesomely tortured Carneys. Soon they stand in the shadows with it and watch the completion of their own Macabre.

During the fruitless search, The Count feels strong impulses to exact private justice on the lawman that continuously reveals his corruption with each step taken. Many hours in, tired of being made a fool; The Count instructs the local to take him and his men back to their camp, as he fears he's putting more lives in danger. During a communal brunch the next day, he informs his company they'll be moving down the road, back in the direction of The City. An investigation will be initiated through a federal outside bureau; The Count has many friends. "The Sheriff will inform me when he locates our lovely Brothers. This place is not safe for us; we'll make camp in The City while digging as deep as I can into what has happened or until we find our Brothers. So please, with only positive thoughts of them being found alive and safe, as quickly as you can, or ever have, take our retreat of fun down! For this place is wicked and undeserving of our services, it's time to move onto safer ground!"

Never has a communal lunch been eaten by this close-knit bunch so quietly, as each can feel the loss already and know a terrible act has taken place. Billy Jones isn't at the meeting. The good man feels broken inside, as though he should have given The Brother's better council before they'd left with the local girls or told on them immediately. There's only guilt for this man, as a foreboding feeling of dread is all that's within. Billy can't show his face; because he feels as though he's truly to blame. The trailer door suddenly opens; the Count is staring at him with the look of a starving wolf. Never has Billy felt this intense type of energy from the Director of Camp. "I'm going to say this once, Billy, if something wickedly evil has befallen our friends, it isn't your fault, their fault, or my fault. The wickedness has stemmed from the ignorance of evil men. Get up; we're heading into the City for reinforcements now!"

The speed of The Count's Carriage as it barely grips the bumpy dirt road is downright scary! The four horses that pull the lavished department are pure muscle and rarely get to run out like this, yet there is no danger of crashing. The extraordinary man that steers them is gifted in many talents. George Wilson protects the Count; he's stood by his side during the search the night before and offered to take the life of the corrupt Sheriff. His boss had refused, as he always has; this is one reason he loves The Count so much. The boss allows those who have the right to practice law to do so.

Billy breathes easier once he steps out of the Carriage and into the bustle of the City. The tall buildings and businesses seem a comfort, whereas usually, they overwhelm him. They enter the City Times, the only paper that matters in this place. The Count is welcomed into an office by a very portly man whose face is covered in parts of the sandwich he's devouring. Upon hearing the story from his longtime friend and supporter, Max Stahl agrees to cover the story and accompany The Count back to Green bud. "I cover what I want, my friend; give me a few minutes, and we'll be on our way."

Next is the Marshall's office. Sam Smith is a scary-looking character; he's almost as big as Leonard, Bill Jones calculates in his mind. "So happens I have some holiday time coming to me, my Count. I'll head this on my own, with my ways of getting to the bottom of this unfortunate matter." "I just hope they're back in camp when we get there." The excellent lawman gives his long time friend a sincere stare; "Green Bud, my Count, Sheriff Dale Birchwood, I'm afraid this most likely didn't end well for your boy's Sir." After stopping at both men's houses, under the guidance of Mr. Wilson, the muscled horses race the Carriage back to camp much quicker than what would be considered safe. There's no talk on the way back, just a hanging tension of evil to come.

The evil Sheriff and a few of his misled henchmen stick out like cobras slithering around a naked baby in a bathtub amidst the organized chaos of the teardown of the Carnival. The Count quickly goes to them, all taking down ceases as the entire camp focuses on the conversation that's about to take place. The surrogate Father knows it's terrible; he feels it in his core.

"Have some bad news, Sir, we found your boys in the woods...." "Hanging around," one of the Sheriff's idiot deputies finishes, causing stunted smiles to form on his crony's faces. The Sheriff takes a moment, as he struggles not to laugh, as he had when he'd seen the Carney's swinging by their necks the night before. "We'll take you there now." "You didn't bring the bodies with you," the Marshall asks? The Count reads the expression on the Sheriff's face; which has turned from antagonist in sorts, to pure frustration. "Marshall Smith, a little ways from home, aren't you?" "I'm on vacation, Dale, and here as a favor to my good friend, The Count, as an overseer to make sure this situation is handled properly." "Boys got to drinking, took a wrong turn, and met some bad folks, or maybe it was your people." "Dale, how about you take us to the bodies, and then we'll want to speak with them, local girls." "Already talked to them Marshall, they pointed us to the spot; where they'd left them hours before." Sam Smith's a man that can only tolerate so much round and round; he seems to grow as he takes a quick step towards the Sheriff. "I'm here unofficially, officially, Dale. This isn't running moonshine, boy. The Count has powerful friends, and unless you want a bunch of us feds down here combing your messy head of hair, you better be square. Now take us out to the woods!" The Sheriff, quickly remembering his place, turns without response and leads his boys back to their horses.

After a short ride, The Count and his party are led deep into the woods. This walk-in itself is dangerous, as these times are savage. Local law is God, and crossing a county line takes power away. Dale Beachwood is smart enough to recognize the quiet man beside this Count, a bodyguard, no doubt, as a dangerous sort. He'd seen Sam Smith take care of business more than once; any thoughts of disposing of this incontinence are dismissed. The squawking of crows soon accompanies a breeze carrying a putrid stench of rot. The dense path being walked quickly gives way to a sunlit opening and a sight that takes Bill Jones to his knees; the vomit is as sincere as the tears that promptly moisten his face. The Count puts a hand on his devastated friend's shoulder as he stares at the tar and feathered bodies of three of the nicest men he'd ever given a chance to, as they swing, hanging from the tree. The Carney leader has a flash of his favorite visuals of The Brothers go through his mind. Memories of them locating lost children or gently helping intoxicated people to a safe place to sit. It's seeing Stitch jammed into the tar-hardened arm of Leonard that almost brings this hardened man to puking as well.

"Girls say they left your fellows here, as they were getting a little too tight for their comfort!" "Un hun," Marshall Smith croons as he begins to walk the scene, carefully examining the surroundings. Within seconds he knows The Brothers were brought here, and certainly not, executed here. In these early Industrial Revolution times, crime scene analysis is not an essential part of an investigation. Still, an experienced lawman like Sam Smith will consider what he has heard, what he sees, and begin to make calculations. No evidence of a party. Many different footsteps are apparent; many more people here than reported. Amazingly, there are no puddles of tar, or excess feathers, marinating the surroundings. Most importantly, there's no evidence that a fire took place here. This strongly suggests that the three ladies who'd lured The Brothers from the Carnival aren't speaking the truth. Smith puts the Sheriff at ease; "Good job in finding the bodies so quickly, Dale. I'm going to concur with you and leave it at that; these boys took a wrong turn somewhere along the line and unfortunately walked into some killing time." The Count watches the Sheriff's face relax; "Just doing my job, Marshall." "My friend here would like the bodies cut down, and we'll take them back, Sheriff...." At that moment, Max Stall pulls the cord of his new camera; there's a bright flash. The crows caw and scatter as the tar stiffened bodies make a cracking sound due to the sudden gust of wind that comes rushing through the clearing. Bill sees bright pins and needles as he looks right into the flash of light. As he turns, now looking back at the atrocity, amidst the partial blindness, he sees the Shadow of a giant cat. Quickly he closes his eyes and shakes his head. Billy lets out a scream when he opens his eyes as the menacing silhouette is now on a branch above the hanging remains of The Brothers. The Count leaves the others, who are now cutting the remains down from the trees. "Billy, are you alright?" "I Just saw a, a...." "Be careful, you red-necked fools," The Count shouts, as one of the Dwarfs has just come crashing down to the ground, sending feathers dancing with the wind! Bill decides to keep his vision to himself, for now, as suddenly he feels a presence, as though he's being watched.

After lamely helping George and Sam tie the remains to the Carriage roof, the local's cops mount their horses and leave without saying goodbye. Their conversation on the way back to town is how stupid the great Marshall Sam Smith really is and how well they played their hand. One of these corrupt humans is much more relieved than the others, as he still has signs of make-up on his face.

The conversation in the Carriage under the tortured couldn't be any different. "Those bastards know theirs a lot more to know Sam," The Count shouts! "Relax, my friend; I know that, you know that, we all know that." "Theirs a much more detailed story for me to write Sammy than the one that crooked badge just forged." "Max, that Sheriff's right in the thick of it. Count, I'm going back to the City to talk to my boss. You need to hold up here while I get reinforcements; this dirt's way too dangerous to start digging around with such few hands. I'll be back by sundown. If I get the green light, we're going to talk to Mayor Jacobs, make us a little deal, and you're going to open shop again. We're going to need to make some friends anyway we can." "This place is rotten, Marshall; I don't want to lose anyone else." The Count puts his hand on the shoulder of his weakened gamesman; "Billy, I know exactly where my good friend Sam is heading with this; sometimes you have to stick your hand right in the bee's-nest if you want the honey."

Before entering the camp, The Count sends Bill inside to get some blankets to cover up The Brothers, as pandemonium is inevitable. Before he talks to his family, The Count knows he needs the solitude of his trailer to regain his composure. Tears are close to breaking through the thin dam he's managed to maintain. All eyes are on the blankets as the Carriage slowly passes through camp. The amusements are put away in their traveling boxes. A sure sign the Carney Brethren is hot to move shop and hopeful their leader would return with The Brothers safely. The sullen and saddened look towards the blankets on top of his Carriage crack that dam. The Count allows himself a moment of weakness in front of The Marshal and the reporter, for he feels this is a safe place, as these men are good friends and good people. Once the Carriage is parked behind The Count's large tent, Sam is given Badger, an animal that lives to run, and he leaves for The City. These men are soon with drinks of whiskey in hand; "To The Brother's," the Count cheers. The boss cries openly in front of Bill Jones, who's unable to drink the whiskey as he's taken back by the compassion of his leader. Billie's not surprised at all. The Count has never had a problem showing his people how much he loves and appreciates them. Anticipation marinates the camp as to what horrors lay beneath the blankets on top of The Count's Carriage. George's been charged with keeping an eye on the Carriage, as well as redirecting his fellow Carney's away, as one after another approaches the boss's tent. Just before sundown, Sam Smith returns with a few other Marshalls; Rodney Teach, Stan Bridges, and Will Blake. Their boss, a man of high morals and justice, has given these lawmen the go-ahead to deal with this barbaric act in any way they see fit. They are without any type of leash. The Count sits up as Smith enters his tent; he puts dignity back in place quickly. The Count solemnly offers whiskey, the new arrivals accept, and over a few snorts, introductions are made. Bill Jones is passed out by the time the men leave to go to the Mayor's house. By this point, Wilson is having trouble keeping the camp in check, as they're all very eager to know what has happened. The Counts stands on the steps of his Carriage and addresses his comrades; "We'll be back soon, my Brothers and Sisters, and all will be revealed. In the meantime, get out the wine and ale, as tonight we'll be celebrating the lives of The Brothers!" Usually, when The Count gives direction to break out the spirits, there's a loud cheer. This close-knit bunch knows they'll never be celebrating with Leonard, Felix, and Joey again.

Mayor Tom Jenkins is a greedy man, a sloth, but in the town of Green Bud, his line is one of the most powerful. A family with a wealthy background in farming, owning thousands of acres. Tom isn't the first Jenkins to have sat at the head of the table in Green Bud, lining his deep pockets off of the sweat of others. Baker lives quite comfortably within a deceitful life lathered in corruption and betrayal. Jenkins is well aware of the situation involving the Carney's who'd gotten feathered. He didn't want to know the details but knows that Carl Hester spearheaded the malice. Hester has done wet work for the Mayor before, eliminating a potential competitor in the beef market. Jenkins views Hester as an expendable instrument that helps to maintain and increase his assets. The Sheriff, another of Tom's errand boys, had told him with confidence that The Marshal and the Carney man were satisfied and that the case was closed. How surprised this wealth-hog is when he opens his front door. The Carney man waits with four other very serious-looking men, who are soon introduced as federal Marshall's. Jenkins immediately picks up the strong scent of whiskey on his unwanted visitors as they walk past him, uninvited, into his sizeable three-storied house. "Shame what happened to your employees sir, I'm sorry they couldn't stay put." The Count, usually a brilliant, diplomatic speaker, has lost restraint due to the quantity of straight whiskey he's ingested. Every cell within directs mouth to act on the impulse from a jaded mind, as he just knows this pig has Intel about his friends, he'll never divulge; "You don't give a damn you bas...." Smith interrupts and puts a hand on his shaken friend's shoulder; "This is just it, Mayor...Jenkin's, I believe, is your name; it doesn't matter. What matters is that my good friend here, The Count has many friends in high places, and one way or the other, we're going to find out what exactly happened to his friends." "I spoke to the Sheriff, Marshal," a pause, and a deliberate chuckle from the overweight have-lot with the messy comb-over; "Sorry, I thought this unfortunate matter was solved. That the Carnival was moving on to more welcoming ground." The arrogance of this pig causes The Count to steam inside. There's a very strange pause. Stan Bridge is a giant who can gently carry one of his eight children to bed, never stirring them from their slumber in the slightest or strike terror into one with a glare. "Listen, fat man, read this, we have jurisdiction, we own this town." The quick movement of the beastly figure causes the Mayor to trip backward into a chair! He's handed a paper signed by the director of the Marshal's office; the article noticeably shakes as it is read. "If you know who did the killing, speak now, Jenkins, and we'll not attach you to the justice we're going to impose; if not, you'll fry in the end. Cause someone always talks to us, boy," Bridges shouts, slamming a fist onto the table! The rich man collects himself for an instant, slowing his entire being down, grabbing for dignity, remembering who he is and where he comes from. "I assure you, I know nothing more than you do of this unfortunate event." "My friend here's going to reopen his Carnival while we conduct our investigation." "That's fine with me...." "We ain't asking, bud," Smith manages. He's ready to pound the truth from a man he knows is well-versed in everything that transpires in the town he leads. The men discuss the Mayor, and all agree that the hog knows much more than he'll ever tell them about the torture and murder on the ride back to the leased land. The sticking point is that the man who'd been so greedy in their initial meeting before setting up; hadn't attempted to renegotiate new terms about reopening the Carnival. "That pig couldn't wait for us to leave Sam!" "We'll take our time and get them all, my Count. This hunt is about patience and applying pressure." The other Marshals agree with their leader, assuring The Count that Justice will be dealt, in one form or another.

When they arrive at The Count's tent this time, the entire camp is assembled outside of it. The blankets have been removed from hiding the gruesome remains of their good friends. These people aren't mad that their leader hasn't spoken to them about what has happened or hasn't moved them from a place that certainly is not safe for them; they are only sad. These humans all know that their director carries a spot deep in his heart for every one of them. Strong loyalty moves each of these souls to only wanting to know what their Count's plans are, as one thing they are sure of, justice will be served. Not one drink has been taken by this unique bunch of misfits, not until their leader says so. The Count isn't ready to talk yet, as he walks towards his tent, with The Marshal's, seeing the tarred and feathered remains of three of his best friends; tears run down his face. He purposely makes eye contact with as many of his children as he can; hurt and vulnerability are on display. Once to the stack of ale and wine, he opens a bottle of the thick merlot, takes a long sip, and yells; "Let's celebrate our fallen Brothers! Tomorrow morning, the Marshal's, and I will tell you how justice is going to be handed down to whoever is responsible for what happened to our dear friends!" The music starts, and the liquor flows; The Count helps serve the booze, showing his love and compassion naturally, and selects those that will tend to build the Pyre for The Brothers. Being chosen for the ritual is considered an honor. The cremation stack is put together in the center of the camp. The bodies are placed on the Pyre. Another large fire is built close by and lit—Carney's dance and cheer, all with fond memories to share about the decency of the fallen.

Bill Jones awakens and stumbles through the dark tent. He feels ashamed and is reluctant to show his face to his Brethren, which he knows has initiated a camp ritual. The Brother's bodies will be given to the darkness soon. The Marble-man smiles when he sees the mood of his Brethren, dancing, smiling, laughing; he sees The Count and goes to his leader. Bill stops as he notices the Pyre and immediately feels as though he's being watched. He looks around for what is stalking him and sees nothing but feels the dark presence from the woods and wonders when the Shadow-Cat will reveal itself. The Count watches Bill stare at the Pyre; knowing him so well, he knows how badly his friend is beating himself up inside, so he goes to him. "Come keep me company while I serve and have a drink, Billy, and remember what I said, son, this isn't your fault. When retribution is dealt, you will not be part of the reckoning; there isn't one here that blames you." Bill takes a whiskey and stands by his leader as he serves. Soon one long-time friend after another comes for more drink, each hugging Bill while assuring him that The Count's words are of the truth and that he has no part in the blame in the wickedness of the men that live on this dirt. Bill drinks whiskey from The Count's bottle, as does the Marshal's. Billy's beginning to relax until he sees the eyes, glowing red, so large, from high above in the trees. Although it's dark, he can see the Shadow with its massive tail swinging as he feels it staring at him. Bill looks to his leader; The Count feels the fear that suddenly comes from his friend. "What's wrong, Billy?" "Do you see that up there in the trees, Sir?" The stutter is rampant. "The smoke, Bill, of course, I know the fire is way too big. Are you alright, sport?" It's the way his gamesman is staring in fright, the sudden paleness of his skin, that spawns alarm. "What should I see, Bill; you were real jumpy. I mean, who wasn't when we saw The Brothers hanging, but you've seen something, haven't you?" During these times, people were much more superstitious and attached to the occult. Most believed in spells and curses; women could still be burned at the stake for being accused of using the dark arts in evil ways to hurt others by way of witchcraft. "It's right there, Count, in those trees, watching me with its giant red eyes, its tail is swinging back and forth; the Shadow...of...fff...aaa...Giant cat!" The Count instructs another to help with drinks; "We'd better go find Lady Dark, Billy." A quick walk through the dancing Carney's proves useless, and as they make their way to the gypsies tent; Bill watches as the giant Shadow follows from a distance, watching him and his master; "It follows us, sir."

Lady dark is the fortune teller to the locals of each town visited by The Never Sleep Swing Company. The lady charges a five-cent piece for each read and gives these clients news they want to hear. Truth is mixed with fantasy. She also sees much darkness around many of the lost souls that pay her, as Lady Dark has the true gift of sight. Her Brethern in the company respects her greatly and knows what an actual burden her life within the occult can be. The lady had warned The Count that they must be cautious in this town two weeks prior. "We can just pass Green Bud, Jane." "We can't boss, what is supposed to be, must be, for there's no way we can hide from what is upon us." The natural Witch waits for The Count and Bill Jones to arrive. She's dressed in her original Wicca threads, necklaces of the ancient, the crystal ball is gone, replaced by her alter of bone and bead. "I've been waiting for you, my friends; take a seat." Jane wears no make-up to hide her very old, unknown age. Her eyes are very blue, and her skin is much wrinkled; she's in the last cycle of her life, the process of knowledge and patience. As Bill and The Count take a seat, they both notice the lifeless body of

Stitch in her lap; "The Shadow of Leonard's pet followed you to my tent, didn't it, Mr. Jones?" Bill nods in agreement. "I've seen the apparition in my dreams, Count; there are people in this town that need to meet a certain group, souls that live in the Shadowland. Our friends, The Brothers, are there now, as they're supposed to be. They have been called on by those that dwell in the darkness. They are now Shepard's to those, whose time has run out, here in the light, and must face the darkness, as they owe blood and pain for the treachery they've committed." The Count does not question; he asks the medium to continue. "The ashes from the cremation will be placed inside of this cat and preserved. I've seen a young girl, who will show herself in the next few days, she will visit you, Bill, and at this moment, all will be revealed during an unexpected victory in your game. I will need blood from each of The Brothers, as well your two favorite marbles Bill." The Count's not surprised that Jane knows the company is staying. The first time they'd met, she'd told him details of his life, which he'd never revealed to anyone. "Go get me you're two favorite marbles, and I'll get the blood that is needed.

While the celebration of The Brother's lives roars during this night, the vessel needed to bring them from darkness to light will be prepared." Bill limps as fast as he can to his game tent; he knows which two cat's eye marbles will be given. As though the round hard objects know their fate, they're the first ones he retrieves from the bucket. As Lady Dark swiftly uses an ancient blade to draw dark blood, the Count watches as the sharp slices through the tarred flesh with ease. After the sacred container is half-filled with the precious donation, the Witch then cuts hair from each of The Brothers that isn't tarred; she places them in an old-looking sac. Although Bill can feel the presence of the Shadow stalking him as he limps to the fire, it's no longer in view; soon, the two marbles are in the hand of Lady Dark; "These are your most precious marbles Mr. Jones?" "They are the most special to me now, Jane. The Brothers gave them to me years ago, and they'd won them in a poker pot." "Very well," The Witch drops them in with the blood of The Brothers and begins speaking in a tongue Bill doesn't understand. Her words are within the ancient. She speaks of loss and love and her devotion to those that dwell in the darkness. Only a few can speak this occulted dialect, none as clear and passionate as Lady Dark, so the ritual begins.

Bill follows his leader back to where the spirits are being served. The company master retakes his place behind the makeshift bar, showing love to all of his valued partners. It takes Lady Dark a few minutes to find Maine Dillard, a special man of many trades, one being taxidermy. The two leave the celebration of their friend's, retreating to the quiet of the Witch's tent. "The Count's okay with all of this, my Lady?" "Absolutely, and he wants it done immediately." "It will be ready by tomorrow night, my Lady." As loyal as any of his fellow Carney's, Maine takes the cat's corpse to his shared tent. The process of preserving Stitch exactly as the Witch has instructed begins. "Maine is taking care of Stitch now. Although the process will not be complete, the animal will eventually be preserved as I've envisioned. Now please, being the best man I've ever known, hug an old lady as we both need one." The tears flow hard once in the embrace of a woman that's helped him become the man he is. The Count had saved her from being burned alive; the good man had risked everything that night, and the true payoff has been the robust moral code that has guided him so surly thus far since. "Be strong, my Count, for, at this moment, these people need you more than ever." Slowly the director lifts his head, his moistened eyes lock with the crystal blue; "I love you, Lady Dark," "And I love you, my Count, now go and speak the words that need to be heard."

With a stool in hand, The Count moves near the power of the fire. He stands on it, rising above his people, and begins speaking from a whole heart. The leader tells his Brethren how he met The Brothers, they've all heard the story, but this version just seems better. The Marshal's and the reporter are introduced, and he tells the camp they're there on their own time, all passionate about making some type of right out of this wrong. The Carney's greet these good men with loud cheers. Next, he describes the scene in which he saw their good friends swinging from the trees, the lack of evidence supporting the Sheriff's lame story, and the strong smell of rot the wind blew under that hot sun. Crying can be heard. "This is why I ask you, my Brothers and Sisters, to risk your lives by staying here! But know this, if you do, justice may be served to those that have brought this darkened moment upon us! Tomorrow, in a state of headaches and weakened stomachs, we'll wake up and bring our Carnival back to life as we patiently wait for those unworthy snakes to be smoked out!" The Count gives Wilson the signal. After a moment of thoughtful hesitation, the bodyguard throws the torch onto the funeral Pyle. The instant the flame takes true life, no longer flirting with the oxygen but seems to take a long deep drag, the orange of the fire explodes into the sky! The strange odor of cooking flesh, marinated in tar and feather, begins to tickle the nasal sense of those that cheer and dance to a song composed for them, the members of, The Never Sleep Swing Company!

Bill Jones suddenly hears the screech of a cat; it's loud, causing him to put both hands over his ears. No one else hears it as he watches them all moving in accordance with the moment. Only Bill registers the screeching as he watches the smoke slither from the bodies of his lost friends. The dark toxins suggest their souls have been darkened by the torturously painful deaths that had befallen them. Bill continues to look for the shadow, the source of the high-pitched screech; it's as if the night has emasculated into one with the dark silhouette.

As the Pyre slowly turns tarred flesh to ash, the celebration of The Brother's lives slows with the sun rising. The last hugs are exchanged before these grief-saturated humans find a place to close their eyes, all filled with the anticipation of the hunt. Lady Dark comes to The Count; "I'll take a good portion of the ash, my Count, as Maine has worked very hard during the wake; you're still fine with what we discussed?" "Have I ever questioned your knowledge of the dark arts, my Lady?" Jane hugs her savior. The Witch puts as much of the Brother's ashes in the container as she feels is needed. As she walks back to the tent, she speaks in the ancient to them, knowing they can hear her in the darkness.

The Count puts his head into a large tub of ice water, the cells of his skin immediately catch up to the fire that burns in his heart. With the help of George, who's one of the few that will not live with a hangover the rest of the day, he gets a large meal prepped for his family. Within a few hours, others begin rising to a welcoming smell of baked beans, frying swine, and coffee. They're greeted by their leader, who is all smiles and gentle touch, hugging each, that takes a portion from George and himself. Max Stahl, who'd met The Count years before, when he first brought the Company to The City, has been moved by the love he'd felt from the Carney's is finding himself having to fight back the tears. The Count nurtures each one of these misfits who could only ever fit into the strange traveling life of a carnival. The bearded woman, the Siamese twin girls, even the gator boy, whose flesh is covered in a peculiar disease, are embraced in a hug. It's as though his friend is a Father consoling his Children after the family dog has been put down. The reporter can feel much more than an article here, theirs a story to tell, and Max knows it's going to take a toll on his being. The Marshal's had bedded down just after the Pyre had been ignited. Now they eat and discuss how they'll proceed with the investigation during the day. They decide they'll personally advertise the reopening of the Carnival in the local taverns, really looking to stumble onto leads. Eventually, they'll pressure the Sheriff into pointing them in the direction of the girls that supposedly left The Brothers in the woods. Each lawman's roles in the interviews are clearly defined, as well as tactics and questioning. While the others wake up and feed, the early risers have already begun rebuilding their mobile park of amusement.

Lady Dark speaks incantations in the foreign tongue as Maine works on Stitch. The hairs of The Brothers have been sewn onto the hairy flesh of the cat. The killers hadn't dipped the animal in tar. Dale thought the cat in its natural state, tucked in the arms of the big one, as his tar and feathered body swung and cracked, would have a much more disturbing effect on the Carneys. Stitches insides had been removed during the night. What is needed to preserve had been added to the corpse with love and attention. Jane decided that the cat would sit up, as though it was watching, as though the cat would always be watching. The marbles will be the cat's eyes; they're resting in the blackened blood and will be added last. The ashes are placed inside to serve as the soul of this vessel to the shadowland.

Word had spread quickly through Green Bud about the murder of the Carneys. The Marshal's first day on the hunt goes cold before it even starts. A clear message has been put out to stay away from the investigating Fed's, as any type of talk would be very dangerous to one's existence in GreenBud.

Michelle Mathers raises unwanted children at the GreenBud orphanage and has decided to ignore the warning she'd received earlier in the day while buying food. This is a woman whose very soul was constructed through and through with empathy. Michelle had cried upon hearing the gruesome details of Carney's murder. A plan had quickly begun to spin in her head, as she'd been told the Carnival would stay in place while the investigation by the Marshal's was carried out. Michelle has always believed that doing good brought about good things for any human. Although her goal of putting the children to work in the kitchen that day making cookies for the Carney's is a genuine action, meant to console, she also sees an opportunity. The orphanage has barely any funding. Taking the fifty-eight children she fends for to the Carnival during the past week is simply not within the budget. She and two other ladies lead the kids to the gates of The Never Sleep swing company that night. Many carry homemade cards that speak of sorry, printed with the imagination of a child who's starved of amusements the gatekeeper sends for The Count. This hardened gatekeeper turns to mush as she's given one of these cards and a cookie from a little girl. "We're all so sorry to hear about your friends Miss." The Count goes directly to the gate to personally welcome the orphans. Sam Smith has made it very clear that their investigation had led nowhere and that they and the camp were considered nothing less than lepers. Also, the girls who'd served as lures as far as the Marshal is concerned have all vanished. Any kind of kindness at this point may be instrumental in finding a lead in the future. Word quickly travels through the camp of the act of kindness, and a small crowd has formed at the gate, all enjoying cookies and reading the homemade cards. The Count manages to maintain his dignity while reading the card he's given. The cookie doesn't mix well with the whiskey he's swallowed, but his heart becomes swollen as he looks into the wanting eyes of the innocent children. "Tonight, you are all our special guests, so come on in and enjoy all we have to offer for no charge, for you are now all friends of The Never Sleep Swing Company." Quickly, The Count gives instructions to shut the gentleman's tent down and close the gate to other potential customers, as the words of Lady Dark have formed into a reality. As these unwanted kids swell with anticipation, in awe of the lights, rides, and smells; the preserved conduit is given to Bill. Although it is still raw, Maine feels his work will hold. Billy places Stitch in the front row with the other homemade prizes. Making the children happy seems to bring peace throughout the camp; their smiles are like pills to fight the depression that has filled them. The usual hustle to make that mighty dollar has been put aside. Never have they operated on a level of pure entertainment to bring pleasure to the lives of abandoned children, as most of the Carney's were as well. Making these poor children happy feels good, honest, and has begun the mending process.

Molly Aiken shyly makes her way through the maze of luring smells and amusement; she'd just arrived at the orphanage the day before and still hasn't made a friend. Bill Jones suddenly hears a screech; he looks in the direction his senses tell him it's coming from. All he sees is a little girl in a tattered brown dress; her dark hair is in two pigtails. "Well, hello, there, my little princess," Molly is too shy to answer back. Bill never stutters when he talks to children. Molly takes her time examining the funny-looking man; his eyes speak of friendliness. Unlike the other children, she hasn't given her card and cookie away yet. Her eyes spot the prizes behind the odd-looking man; it's the stuffed cat that steals her attention, and as though Stitch is directing her, she hands Bill the card. There's a drawing of three stickmen holding hands with a colorful rainbow in the background; it's very well done. Once opened, the message reads, "May your friends find peace." Bill takes a bite of the cookie as tears run down his face; "My game is all about getting a marble to land and stay in one of these dishes; how about you throw as many marbles as it takes to win one." Molly smiles at Bill; she feels excited for the first time in a long time. Life hasn't shown this one much joy as of yet. The gamesman opens up his hand, offering the little girl some marbles. His intention is for her to take them all, offering many tosses, as he knows it will take her a while; she only takes one. Molly studies the beautiful round object; poverty has prevented her from most experiences other children take for granted; she tosses it without thought. "You need to aim...." Bill begins, and then he hears the loud smack of the marble hitting the plate. When he turns, he sees a first in all of his years of running this hustle; the marble has cracked the middle dish, always the greasiest! His routine is an obsessive compulsion to grease the center dish last and always with the heaviest slicks. The crack suggests the shot stuck to the heavy glass as though magnetized by an unseen force. Bill turns back to the little girl, his eyes widened as in the background, the dark shadow of the cat is on the wall of a white tent about twenty feet directly behind. He hears purring; the presence is dark yet welcoming. He's about to talk up Stitch, feeling the little girl may want something more fun-looking, but before he can speak, Molly points directly at Leonard's dead pet. The shadow cat watches Billy hand the conduit to the child; "This cat once belonged to an excellent friend of mine; its name is Stitch." Molly smiles at Bill; she hugs her new best friend, "I'll take good care of him, Mister." Without saying goodbye, she walks away, barely able to carry Stitch, as he's almost as big as she. Bill's skin crawls in the creep as he watches the dark shadow slither behind her, strutting as though it's guiding a cub. Bill goes to Lady Dark very quickly, her tent is closed, and he tells her what has just happened; "It has begun, Bill." "What has begun, Jane?" "The afterlife of our Brother's Bill. Their search for justice to be brought upon those that have it coming. The deserving who think they've gotten or are getting away with it."

A few hours later, the camp closes, as all wish the orphans a good night at the gate. How badly the Carney's wish every night was as pure as this one had been. Pleasuring the orphans has been nothing less than a cleansing of their souls. There's no drinking on this night, as all feel satisfied, better, and are very tired from the night before. As the camp seems to rest at once, Max Stahl begins to write. The reporter has been genuinely moved once again by what he's witnessed on the leased land. As he begins to write what has started in the jaded town of Green Bud, the supernatural phenomena he will document, the story flows through him as though he'd written it before.

Molly Aiken's eyes open; she is on her new cot, near the bottom left corner of the large room that sleeps all 58 children. She can't move. There's a weight on her chest. She can hear purring and feel kneading, as though there are two tiny paws gently pushing into her little chest. Molly tries to sit up but can't; she's paralyzed, her heart rate races! The gentle kneading gets heavier as the little girl slightly feels nails penetrating her pajama top, scratching at her flesh. Molly feels energy through her nerve endings; it burns! The weight becomes heavier and heavier upon her chest; she can barely breathe. Molly sucks in hard, closing her eyes to the darkness, feeling as though she's about to suffocate, and hears a loud pop! Upon opening her eyes, she's looking at herself in bed as she's standing beside her cot. Molly sees her body on the bed, with the shadow of a cat sitting on her chest, her head is erect, and her body completely straight and stiffened. Her prize sits at the foot of her bed, staring at the shadow that gently kneads her flesh. Molly scans the room; the other children are asleep, she calls out, but none of them stir. Molly then sees the three dark shadows standing in the corner; one is very large, the other two are small, and their backs are to her. Slowly the dark figures turn in sequence; their eyes are glowing red! Molly wants to run; she's scared. She tries to scream to awaken the other orphans, but they do not respond. As the shadows are almost upon her, the girl feels the cat gently rubbing against her legs. The shadow cat seems to be showing her affection, trust; she watches the cat jump into the arms of the giant. It gently strokes the dark silhouette with its massive shadowy hand. Molly then feels each of her hands taken by the smaller ones. Their touch is cold, and there's an odor of decaying rot; yet their presence is of peaceful needing, as though they're asking her for direction. What this little girl doesn't know is that these are the three men she'd heard about, the tortured ones, the men she'd drawn holding hands by the rainbow. Soon the spirits of the dead form to the living. Caught between a supernatural plain between her world and their world, they float out the door, into the shadows. For as long as Molly Aiken lives, she will serve as a compass to the Shadowmen.

Chapter 2

Laura Sworn gets off the bus; she's tired and wants to sleep; however, today is her daughter Jessica's sixteenth birthday. Laura promised herself that before she takes her illegal opiates, she would make her daughter pancakes for breakfast. Laura's night shift at the nursing home had been a very long and difficult one for her and her coworkers, as a G.I. outbreak had been declared earlier in the day. The residents infected are suffering from vomiting and incontinent loose bowel movements. Laura's a housekeeper at the True Care nursing home; her focus is to get into the corners, whereas the day-time cleaning staff takes care of the broad strokes. Laura makes the home a-septic, sterile, a vital part of long-term care; viral infections kill seniors. This woman takes her job very seriously, which means she works hard every shift. Although the high-rise project she lives in is dangerous, "Broken Pavement," as this ghetto building is referred to, is also peaceful in an obtuse way early in the morning. The graffiti and broken needles seem to sway to the barely audible hip hop bass that slithers through the air as the sound faintly escapes the apartments that house so many broken souls. Laura is the minority in this project. Her white skin calls out as if she were a pink zebra in the middle of the herd; she and her Mother and daughter seem to go unnoticed. It's as though their different color excludes them from the dangerous game that exists in this hostile ecosystem. Laura has been mugged in the past, as well as her apartment was burglarized. Her lawless neighbors had learned long ago that there was no point in dipping the bucket into the well if it's dry. The white lady's also a valued customer of The Road Crew Mafia. Laura's addicted to morphine, and She pays cash every time. Laura takes the drug when she needs to sleep between shifts. The time frame is sixteen hours; she sleeps for eight and wakes up just after Jessica comes home from school. This hardworking single Mother has tried many sleeping pills over the years, only to feel like a zombie that never dreams, thus never achieving proper R.E.M. sleep. A former coworker on the midnight shift had introduced her to heroin. The small amount Laura spikes has never increased; therefore, it hasn't become a burden yet. Laura's Mother is completely outer limits, as she's marinated through and through with dementia. Most of the time, it's a funny, gentle possession. However, delirium is triggered by paranoia, a complete block to who she's around and where she is causes chaos. If not for her drug plan at True Care, she couldn't afford her Mother's medication. The slight taste of smack keeps her even. It allows her to continue on the relentless grind of which is her life.

Once again, the dirty elevator is broken. After a long walk up the polluted stuffy stairwell, which has a very dark history of every crime imaginable, this tired lady finally gets home. A five-minute shower helps with a second wind. Laura begins her motherly duties in the kitchen, highly motivated to put a good meal in her very unspoiled daughter's belly. Jessica takes care of so much for her and does so without acknowledgment; her girl never complains. Jessica does what she has to, and this is why their difficult life works.

Jessica wakes up to the loud buzz of her alarm; she's excited as the smell of her birthday breakfast is quite evident. The dark-haired, brown-eyed girl doesn't anticipate a magnificent gift, just the half an hour her Mother and she will spend together while she enjoys the homemade blueberry pancakes. Sure enough, there's a stack waiting for her at the table. The teen sits across from her Mother, whose eyes seem to be trapped in the dark rubber of tiny tires, making her look so weak; "Happy birthday Jess." "Mom, you look so tired. This is great, but why don't you get some sleep." "Not even if doing so would retire me ten years sooner, Jess," they both laugh, as the response is part of the yearly ritual. "How was work, last night Mom?" "Very demanding, Hun; as it always is, work is work. This is why you have to stay focused. That scholarship to City College isn't going to just hand itself to you, my dear." "Ninety-four percent on my biology exam, Mom." Laura gets up and walks in pain to her daughter; she gives her a big hug. "I'm so proud of you, Jess." She pulls away, looking into her daughter's brown eyes that suggest a life of discipline. Not the excitement of a typical sixteen-year-old that has the world to discover in front of her. "Any boy's Jess, you're sixteen now?" "There are lots of boys, Mom, but they ignore a girl like me, one that's always got her face buried in a book. I guess that's why they never see me." Between studying on breaks and being in class at high school, Jessica Sworn might also be sleepwalking in the halls of the school as she floats through her existence like a ghost.

After breakfast and another genuine hug from a proud Mother, Jess has a quick shower and gets ready. On her way out the door, her Mother informs her that the elevator is broken again. It's a slow walk down the stairs, as many inhabitants of Broken Pavement are now up and moving towards both legal and illegal work.

Jessica barely gets to the bus stop on time. She will read ahead of where they are in class during the hour and ten-minute commute; every second counts to this humble young lady. Jessica has much bigger dreams than cleaning up after incontinent elders.

Laura checks on her Mother, who is still sleeping; she'd always been a late sleeper. According to Jess, her temperament had been very even the night before and very receptive. Granny was talkative, continent, and most importantly, no paranoia at all. Laura decides to leave her pills for her with a glass of O.J. The dealer told her that it was a new mix when Laura had stopped a few floors down to score the junk before working the night before.

The tired woman carefully looks for a good vein between her toes as she sits on the edge of her bed. She doesn't flinch as she pushes the needle into her flesh. The warm flow of utopia is instant, as the drug is potent, hot, and its temperature rises as it slithers through her being. Laura takes a deep breath, and that's when she feels the pop in the middle of her chest. This loving Mother slides into the darkness as she lays face down in her vomit. The heroin hadn't been cut enough; this true heart has been boiled by the intensity of the junk's purity.

Just as Jessica readies herself for lunch, she's paged through the intercom to come to the office. The vice-principal has been in this situation too many times and isn't nervous at all. Giving bad news to these students is expected in this place "Your Mother has passed away, there's a police car waiting for you, Miss. Sworn, to take you home; apparently, your Grandmother is very out of sorts." "Dead, well, what's happened? This can't be right. She just made me breakfast for my birthday!" The V.P. has to take a second as she tries to maintain dignity, only wanting to move past this moment. The teenager's body shakes. She's in shock, so she puts a hand on Jessica's shoulder; "I don't know the details, but it certainly sounds like your Grandmother is going to need you; there isn't much else I can say. You're going to have to do what you're going to have to do, Miss. Sworn. The police cruiser is out front; good luck." The Vice-principal, minutes later, is crying in her office, revaluating her approach. It's been some time since she'd watched actual innocence be so abruptly assaulted. As if in a trance, Jessica walks through the herd of students who rush through the hall. None of these kids take notice of the tears streaming down her face, nor will they notice that Jessica will never return, for she's finished hiding in these halls.

Chapter 3

J essica sits in the main foyer of "The Your Care," retirement home, beside the Director-of-care's office, Martha
Brown. The D.O.C. has been nothing short of a godsend
for the broken teen, who hasn't been to school in four days.
Upon getting home and shortly after watching her Mother's
corpse get wheeled out of their small apartment, her Grandmother had to be sedated. Jessica called the home, not knowing what else to do. Martha, her voice sounding devastated, had
told her she'd be right over. From the moment Jessica had met
the good lady in the parking lot, not wanting her Mother's boss
to walk up the stairs on her own, the D.O.C. has taken care of
everything. Laura had a minimal life insurance policy; Martha
made arrangements for the cremation and then set up a wake in
one of the entertainment rooms of the retirement home. All the
food and drinks provided for. Her Mother had been very well-
liked. Almost everyone that worked at the facility had shown up,
whether they were working or had the day off. It was pretty evident that her Mother's untimely death had affected the atmosphere of the home. Many of her fellow employees, in tears, had
shared fabulous stories about Laura and her genuine dedication
to her work. The wake had a true feeling of sadness, for a life lost
way too early and was sure to be missed. Martha had also made
sure that Jessica's Grandmother had her medication adjusted.
She'd set up a free doctor's appointment through the home the
day she'd come to Broken Pavement. The registered nurse had

brought a needle with her, and after injecting Grandma, she passed out. Just as Martha had promised, after the small cost of the cremation, there was enough money left over from the life insurance Jessica and her Grandmother to live off for about three months. Without this money, Jessica and her Nan would have been split up. Both would have been put under the government's protection; these types of facilities are infamous for doing more damage than good.

Right at the end of the wake, Martha had made a beautiful speech. The D.O.C. spoke of the people Jessica's Mother had touched at Your Life. How they'd remember her for her hard work ethic, empathy, and genuine willingness to put her own needs behind the needs of the residents. Martha stayed clear in her speech of the unfortunate way Laura had accidentally ended her own life. The room was filled with sounds of hurt and loss that harmonized with Martha's touching speech. She'd finished it with, "Jessica, all of us have decided that we'd like to offer you, you're Mother's job. We all know how hard of a worker you are. Your Mom was always telling us how you take care of your Grandma and the outstanding grades you earn. We all know what a difficult spot you're in. I've assumed that maintaining your life in that apartment with your Grandmother is what you will pursue, so we here at Your Life would like to make this easier. I know you're only sixteen and had plans to go to college, but we would love for you to come to work with us, assuring that eventually, you will reach your goals." The grieving teenager had accepted on the spot. Jess had felt the thick texture of stress peel from her entire being. All of those in the room had cheered, and one by one congratulated her with hug after hug. A neighbor down the hall from the Sworn's apartment, Cynthia, had agreed to watch Grandma while Jess was trained and would eventually work.

Martha opens her door; she quickly shakes off the anger she's feeling from dealing with the miserable child of one of the residents. Unfortunately, the woman has many false expectations of what her Mother is capable of. Martha, who's been in the nursing business for years, understands the woman's frustration; but still hasn't gotten used to being spoken to this way. Jessica's nervous. Although Martha told her the interviews a formality, she's used to being let down. Jess is waiting for a reason why she won't get the job at the home. "We all took a guess, Jessica, at your size, small, and bought you these five pairs of scrubs." The teen starts crying; "Jessica, easy," the nurse hugs her friend's daughter. "No one's ever been this good to me, Martha, what you and the others have done, I can't believe it, I mean...." "Your Mother meant a lot to all of us, Jessica. As in her co-workers and the residents that know what is going on, she touched all of us. You're signing papers that will start your journey today; you're one of us now." The papers are signed; Jessica's given a nametag and then shown to the change room, where she's given a locker. "Put a pair of those scrubs on Jessica, and when you're done training today, get yourself a good pair of shoes. Suitable footwear is essential to maintaining your entire body in this business. You're going to take many steps on these unforgiving floors, and over time your body will feel the punishment it is sure to absorb.

Jessica changes into the pink scrubs and puts the nametag on. She looks at herself in the mirror; a feeling of pride washes over her. The teen feels as though she's honoring her Mother. "Jessica, I'm Lynn; we met at your Mom's wake. I'm going to train you today. I'm quite excited, and let me say if you're half as good and strong as your Mom was, this is going to be a breeze for you." After a handshake that evolves into a genuine hug, the older woman shows Jess to the staff lounge, and she puts on the Your Life training video for her. "Here's the test that you must get 70 percent on, to pass Jess. Feel free to fill it out as you watch it; it's just a formality." Feeling as though the video is a window into her Mother's other life, Jessica is entranced by it. She finds the two-hour instructional seminar about housekeeping to be quite fascinating. Jess quickly answers the fifty-eight multiple-choice questions, scoring a hundred percent.

It's as though this job is embedded in her D.N.A. Over the next five hours, Lynn, who's doing this on her day off, will show

Jessica her routine. Very quickly, it becomes evident that Laura's daughter is a quick study and eager to please. Lynn's given much training over the years and never has a newbie picked up so much from the training video alone. They're through the introduction checklist in a few hours, allowing for the advanced technique in keeping a sterile environment to commence a day early. "Jessica, you're going to be a major asset to this home; if you work like this on your own on the midnight shift, your Mother would be so proud."

After walking Laura's daughter to the front door, Lynn hurries to her boss's office; she's very excited. "There's no way she stopped that video once to answer any of the questions. Jess was done in two hours and twenty minutes, Martha, and what she'd picked up just from watching the video was terrific. Jess reminded me about a few things I'd forgotten. I can assure you that giving Jess this job will not be looked upon as charity; she's going to be a powerful asset to our home just like Laura was. The boss is thrilled.

Jessica gets off the bus, one-stop before her usual drop-off in front of Broken Pavement. The teen tries not to think about her Mother as she goes into the sports store to buy shoes; instead, she focuses on her training day. Jess had genuinely enjoyed learning from Lynn, and she'd been paid for the first time in her life. A young man soon approaches her and asks her if he can help. Jessica describes what her job will entail, quoting Lynn how unmerciful the floors in the home are. A few minutes later, a pink and white pair of jogging shoes have her complete attention. They cost one hundred and twenty dollars; she's never owned shoes worth more than thirty bucks. After a few yards walked in the sneakers, she splurges. Jess decides to break in her new runners by walking home rather than riding the bus. Her new kicks are so comfortable that Jess feels like she's floating; she never asked her Mom to spend that type of money on footwear or any clothing for her. Grief and guilt quickly wash over her; the teen's unable to fight back the tears. Shoes, she thinks to herself, feeling as though she doesn't have the right to be happy anymore.

The loud hip-hop music can be heard blasting from the court-yard of Broken. Jessica puts her head down as if the motion will turn her into an unnoticed shadow that will go unnoticed. These unworthy humans run many different hustles in the courtyard, from hooking to gang banging, slinging rock, and robbing are all entangling throughout this graffiti-covered concrete jungle. There's little respect for the true gift that human life is. Jessica ignores the catcalls that come from various directions. Most of these lost souls do not know, nor could they care less, that her Mother has just died from an overdose. Jess doesn't risk waiting for the elevator and heads straight for the stairs. A few floors up, she's forced to stop as two drunken teens fight. One of the boys had hit on a girl that the other one had been crushing on, as the larger one is putting it. Jess manages to go around them; she takes some spit on the side of her face from one of the degener-ates. Both teens are in complete need of belts, as their pants are moments away from losing the battle being forged with gravity. "Watch where you're going bitch, or I'll toss your white ass down the stairs!" Jess doesn't dare reply, as killers are bred young in this place. "I'd stick it in that ugly whore," she hears one of them comment, both laugh. "Glad I could mend broken fences," she thinks to herself.

Upon opening the door to her floor, Jess is immensely relieved to see no one in her hallway. As she puts her key in the door, her Grandmother's very old music can be heard. The teen enters the apartment and is greeted by Cynthia, who's sitting at the kitchen table enjoying vodka and orange juice. "You're Nan's had a bad day, Jess. She refused to use the washroom or eat. She's just sat in her chair staring at the white fuzz on the T.V., talking to her-self, and laughing all day." Jess isn't upset or surprised. Quickly she makes arrangements with her neighbor, and they say their goodbyes.

Jessica goes into the living room and finds Grandma staring at the T.V. as the white fuzz on the screen hums; she's giggling like a little girl. "Enjoying your programs, Grandma?" "Jessie, baby, how was school?" Jessica goes to her and hugs her; she's soaked in her urine. "School was fine, Gran." "I've had the most wonderful day Jess. I've discovered this grand show about a carnival, it's wonderful. There are three brothers; they've been talking to me as they do their work, making all the kids so happy. They want to give me a job, take me on the road with them." "That sounds great, Nan." "I can smell the cotton candy, Jess." "I'm sure you can Gran, you must be hungry." "They fed me, Jess." "Let's go to the bedroom and get your pajama's on, and then we'll have some soup, okay, Gran." Jessica feels her Grandmother's cold hand clench her wrist; "Your Mother must be working a double shift, and you know what, she didn't call to tell me." "We'd better go to bed early, so it's quiet when she gets home, okay, Nan?" As Jessica gets her Grandmother ready for bed, she knows she will not be returning to high school, as her life is no longer the priority.

The still darkness of her room transports Jessica's mind back to the moment she'd watched her Mother's corpse being rolled out of the apartment on that gurney. Jess manages to fall asleep, crying, as the haunting image replays over and over in her mind. Less than an hour later, she's aggressively dragged from her slumber by the loud bangs of gunfire; screaming follows! The incident seems to have occurred very close, a floor down and not far up the hallway from where she lays. The shooting isn't unusual for Broken Pavement, as lives are taken every week in the low rental concrete slum. Soon the flashing lights of emergency response vehicles will slither their way into the windows of the apartment.

The government employees will go through the motions, as they're aware that the residents of Broken Pavement seem to misplace their tongues during these tragic events. Jessica gets up to go to the bathroom; she hears her Grandmother happily talking away as she passes her open door. Jess decides she will ask her if she needs to use the washroom. "Jessica, look at my new pet. Isn't she a beautiful cat?" The teen doesn't reply; she can only stare in disbelief at her Grandmother, who's sitting up with perfect posture on the edge of the bed. Her body language suggests the animal is resting on her shoulder while rubbing its head against her Grandmother's. "She's so friendly, dear;" suddenly, her Grandmother tries to stand! On impulse, Jessica rushes towards her; "Easy, Jess, you'll...." Irene lets out a scream as she feels the cat's claws that she can only see dig deep into her chest! Just as Jessica manages to steady her, the unseen animal jumps from her grip! "Jessica, you've frightened her, and she's scratched me. You never rush towards someone who's holding an animal; you should know better!" "I'm sorry, Grandma, how about we just lay back down in bed," frantic, the elder pushes past her Granddaughter! "I have to find her, Jessica. I told the three Brothers from the Carnival that I'd watch her well they took care of some business. The giant one sure loves his cat." As though her legs have mutated into those of a twenty-year-old, Irene rushes from the room. Jessica follows her around the apartment, shocked, as her Grandmother's gait is nothing short of unreal.

The sudden attack of delirium doesn't allow her Grandmother's confused mind to register fatigue. After an hour of following her aimlessly about, Jessica decides she'll give her Grandmother an injection from one of the needles Martha had given her. Jess hates to do so, but she'll not allow this risky search to continue, as she fears that a broken hip is sure to be the end result. "She's on the couch Jess!" Lenore screams, suddenly changing her direction! Visually the scene is unreal, impossible! Her Grandmother's about to pick up the hallucination that compels her; Jess firmly wraps her arms around her! She sits her on the couch. This isn't easy, as Granny's muscles are fueled by her fight gland, and the full force to maternally defend is the source of this hybrid energy. After a bit of a struggle, Jessica manages to inject her; the effect is simultaneous. "I hope the Brothers aren't going to be mad at me, I...." Jessica lays her Grandmother on the couch and covers her up; she makes coffee and sits on the recliner. The teen mentally prepares herself to keep watch all night and then go to work the next day. Exhausted youth doesn't make it as she finds herself in a trance, staring at the changing lights of the emergency vehicles that are in the parking lot.

Jessica is woken hours later, as her shoulders are being shaken. Her eyes slowly come through the haze, and her Grandmother's face is inches away; her hot breath is so bad. Long scraggly white hair is tickling the teen's skin; "The Brothers found her for me, Jess. They told me not to worry but that I do need to have my wound cleaned!" "Just give me a minute Gran, let me wake up...." Jessica cuts her response as her Grandmother pulls down her nightgown, revealing a deep scratch. "What have you done, Grandma?" "I didn't do this, child; the cat did it when you rushed at me!" Jessica rushes to the medicine cabinet. Granny's right on her heels! "How does she remember this," Jess thinks, as her Grandmother's short-term memory is all but gone. Irene doesn't move or react to the cleansing agent as it foams viscously on the nasty wound. Jessica feels she must have used a fork; she decides to hide the utensils right away. "The Brothers still trust me, Jess, and they would like me to watch their cat again tonight. They specifically asked that you not scare her again, okay Jess?" "Gran, I will give both you and the cat space." "That's all we ask Jess;" Irene gives her Granddaughter a hug and a kiss; "Has your Mother called yet? Is she working another shift?" "She has Gran; they're going to need her for a while. Mom told me to tell you she loves you very much and to be careful while I'm at school today." The elderly woman smiles and winks at her; "Anything you say, Jess."

Cynthia accepts Jess's offer to watch her Grandma for a liter of vodka and mix when she is at work. The older woman is retired and spends most of her time shut in her apartment watching T.V. and drinking. It's cheap sitting, but more importantly, Jess trusts Cynthia, as she's been a good neighbor and had been friends with her Mother. "Call me if she gets terrible. Just make sure she takes her meds." "Got you, you look tired, girl." "I don't have time to be tired, Cyndi."

Jessica runs into the police on the stairs. The detective stops her; he's the only one not in uniform. Jessica's seen the big man before; he's handsome with his coco skin and light blue eyes.

According to his age, his parent's relationship would have been frowned upon in the days of his conception. Detective Smith pushes her hard. He could have let her leave after her pre-programmed response of not hearing anything or seeing anything, but he's tired of this routine. Smith intends to go door to door with the uniforms to ensure nobody has seen anything in the projects he'd grown up in. Smith is dedicated to protecting life as it exists within this concrete jungle. The Road Crew mafia runs the black market business in these jaded halls, and Smith will look hard for that one person willing to open their mouth and do the right thing. "You didn't even hear the gunshots; what did you say your name was again?" "Jessica Sworn." "Jessica, have you heard of The Road Crew Mafia?" "You'd have to be deaf not to have." Jessica wants to shout into the face of this intimidating man; she doesn't. She knows that this man can make her life very difficult and that corrupt cops exist within this savage ecosystem. "Boss can I have a minute;" Smith walks up the stairs. The big man has a different energy when he comes back to her; "Sorry to hear about your Mother kid, liked her junk a bit too much, well anyways, sorry. If there's anything you do remember, the drugs that took your Mother's life probably are indirectly involved with what...." "I don't care, that's none of my business, just like whatever happened last night isn't, and every other day in this toilet. I have nothing to say to you, so can I go to work?" The detective is as surprised as Jess by her sudden assertiveness. He likes her, a smart kid, he thinks to himself, satisfied, she knows nothing. "By all means, Jessica, and I am sorry to hear about your Mother. I look forward to being a part of the justice that may be served on her behalf someday." Jess manages a smile, as she knows this man must be frustrated, trying to do an impossible job.

While waiting for the bus, Jessica looks at her new shoes. She feels the material of the new scrubs on her skin, a uniform, the same job her Mom had. As the tears come, the teen feels a deep sense of pride; she hopes her Mom sees her and is proud.

Lynn waits for Jess; she's having a cigarette by the bus stop.

"Waiting for me, Lynn?" "I have to leave the property when I endeavor in this nasty habit, so I thought I'd wait for you; how are you doing?" Jessica fills Lynn in on what has happened since they'd last seen each other. The older woman doesn't know what to say. She'd heard stories about the Broken Pavement Highrises; it was a topic Laura had always wanted to avoid when the two of them had worked together. "You haven't slept, Jess?" The teenager shakes her head no; "Martha will understand. I mean, you did well yesterday; I'm sure she would let you go home." "I feel better being here already like this place is a break, an escape Lynn. Besides, my Mom did this for years and never complained about the routine to me; she did what she had to, and so will I. I don't intend on letting any of you down; you guys have been amazing." Lynn believes every word the teen has spoken, as Jessica is her Mother's daughter.

Lynn lets Jessica lead, as though they're doing a mock run-through of what the girl's nightly duties will be. Jessica breezes right through it, not missing an angle. It's as though she's an actress that's been rehearsing her lines for days. Upon hearing about the successful training, Martha gives Lynn permission to spend the rest of the shift introducing Jess to the residents of the Westwing, where she'll be working. The teen is nervous upon meeting the first resident but relaxes as soon as Tom Sanders tells a corny joke; Jess bursts out laughing! It isn't the simple joke that gets her. It's his checkered pants pulled up to his chest, accompanied by a brutal comb-over that's failing to hide the baldness that has taken over his head. The war vet catches her staring at his hair; "You know Jessica, grass doesn't grow on a busy street," and he points at his head. "You're amazing," she scream-laughs, shaking her head at Lynn. Soon Tom is showing her pictures. Jessica's in awe, taking in this older man's wisdom and his clear instructions not to be touching his things if she must come into his room. "Your Mother was a special lady Jessica; she was very proud of you. We'd talk at night when I couldn't sleep; I hope you'll do the same for me." Jessica instinctively wraps her arms around Tom; "I look forward to it, Mr.

Sanders."

Lynn warns Jessica to wash her hands and that too much contact with the residents isn't always good. "Your primary function is to stop the spread of bacteria Jess, I'm not pulling a power trip, but as sweet as Mr. Sanders is, he's incontinent. Tom likes everyone to think he is, just like he thinks he's fooling other residents with that comb-over." "Got you, Lynn, thank you." Slowly and genuinely, they work their way through the large Wing. Jessica feels her ribs beginning to hurt with each visit, as these extraordinary people bring her so much joy.

The residents that are competent of mind speak very highly of her Mother. Jessica hears stories about how her Mom helped them, did favors. These small tasks would seem easy to a young person. Still, to an older person, they are stressful; little things such as resetting a cable box or finding a channel on television. Some of the residents are sedated or plain lost, but Lynn takes her time with them, and some react to Jessica, seeming to grasp her youthful energy. These visits are just as rewarding, even if they only produce a faint smile from the impaired, and then they get to the last room on the left, sixty-seven.

"Molly doesn't like company, Jess." "Does she get angry, Lynn?" "Not exactly...she doesn't speak to us; she's catatonic. Molly allows us to bathe her, feed her, as she quietly exists. Between you and I, Jess, Molly's very creepy." "Is she sick?" "That's just it, medically; she's fine. The doctors have no understanding of her condition. All involved with her care feel her refusal to speak is behavioral. For months Molly doesn't speak, and then she randomly says something to one of us. Her speech is perfect, and usually, what she says is very personal to that of the one she's spoken to." "Did my Mom talk to her at all?" Lynn takes a minute, as though trying to give an appropriate answer; "You need to spend as little time as possible in her room at night, Jessica. There's no immediate need for you to go in their Jess. Molly gets up and uses the toilet when she wants, yet she must be pushed down to the dining room in a wheelchair and fed. I don't take anything residents do personally, Jess, and I try my hardest never to speak poorly of them. They're all near the end of their lives and under an incredible amount of stress. Your Mother treated the residents with this type of respect; however, she'd have agreed with me when I say something very dark surrounds Molly Aiken. It's as though she's never alone in that room. It's as if a spirit or a presence is always watching her and those that are near her." It's Lynn's eyes that cause her skin to crawl; they speak of sincerity, of being scared, as though the older woman is issuing a grave warning. Martha approaches them, "Molly Aiken, she's a unique individual. I'm sure Lynn's been filling you in, Jessica." The D.O.C. opens the door and points Jess into the room; her manager asks her to be quiet. Lynn signals to Martha that she'll wait in the hall.

The room is dark, as the curtains are closed. A small night light allows Jess to see her surroundings barely. Molly sits on the edge of her bed; she wears a blue hospital gown, her long grey hair falls past her waistline. There's no furniture in the room, just a small dresser. On top of the dresser sits a stuffed black cat; it's in a sitting position. Jessica stares into the piercing marbles that serve as its eyes; she feels the darkness Lynn was talking about. The cat's piercing-marble-stare seems to be following every step the teenager takes. "Hello Molly, it's Martha. I want to introduce you to someone; this is Jessica, Laura's daughter." As her back is to them, neither sees the raised whites of Molly's eyes snap back to the sky color of blue; the older woman feels the robust switch of energy in the room. Martha and Jessica jump back, startled as Molly's body violently snaps backward into a stuck, impossible angle! Her rigid upper torso, seeming to float about ten inches off the bed. Although the position is quite possible, visually, it's surreal. Only Molly can see the silhouette of Stitch slowly move back and forth on the wall. She's waited for the shadow to reveal itself to her while she's awake for a very long time. The resident lets out a high-pitched giggle as her body remains suspended in the awkward. Jessica feels tiny dormant hairs rise while tickling her skin. Martha's fascinated by the occult and stares with much curiosity within. Not much is known about the past of Molly Aiken. However, there's no doubt in the Director of Care's mind that the older woman has spent a good portion of her life immersed in the dark arts. Jessica feels Lynn's warning; she's terribly frightened and would like to leave the room. Suddenly Molly's blue eyes are upon her. Her face is smothered in wrinkles that suggest a life that hasn't been easy. In a voice that touches on demonic, high and low at the same time, Aiken speaks, "You know Jessica; they either get Stitched or Kneaded." After looking hard into the eyes of this new form of energy, Molly turns away and slowly raises her head; her eyes flip back up to the whites, unseen by the visitors. Martha gives Jess a "let's go" nod. Molly's never addressed her or anyone else that works at the home by their first name. It's only ever been documented that occasionally the resident will speak randomly creepy sentences to the staff.

The D.O.C. can't wait to talk to her good friend, who also has an intense intrigue with the occult about what she'd just witnessed. "You know Jessica, they either get Stitched or Kneaded." The words spoken in that evil tone run through her mind over and over. Martha's in a hurry, as she needs to get back to her office to document what she'd had just seen. "Lynn, thank you for doing a great job with Jessica; there's no doubt in my mind that she's ready and will be on task. Good luck tomorrow night, Jess. Write me a message and put it through the mail slot in my office door if you have any problems." She gives Laura's daughter a good hug and leaves. Martha documents the strange event in detail. The registered nurse is as passionate about the occult as she is about nursing. On her own time, very privately, Martha's been observing humans close to death for years; the dying see things that others do not. Martha's obsessed with getting into the head of Molly Aiken and learning what she knows. What keeps her in this altered state of consciousness. Most importantly, what accompanies her while alone in the darkness of her room. Excited, she calls her friend and makes plans to discuss the new developments later that night.

Jessica will take Lynn's advice by spending as little time as possible in room sixty-seven. Although crossing through the Broken courtyard is much more dangerous to Jesse's life than Molly Aiken, the teen does it effortlessly. Forty-ounce beers mix with the strong scent of pot, as these broken adults pay no attention to setting a good example for the impressionable youth that play. Many of these lost humans are without a shirt. Their muscle's strong of which the butts of many guns can be seen resting on. Jessica pays no attention as the catcalls commence; she looks forward to a good night of watching T.V. with her Grandmother and an early sleep.

The elevator's in service. Jessica gets to her apartment door unscathed; the energy inside appears to be tranquil. Cynthia sits at the kitchen table, a book lies open on its front, about half-read. The vodka bottle near empty validates the older woman's voice, which is slightly hindered in its delivery. "Your Grandmother's had a good day. She's sat on the couch staring at the blank T.V., engaged in many conversations with three brothers only she can see. It's bizarre and very creepy, but the vodka helps with that." "She's used the bathroom, Cindy?" "Many times, by herself, dear. I'll go now to the sanity of my apartment to finish my vodka." A time is agreed upon for the next night, and money for a new bottle is given. Cindy's far from cut, as the older woman's gait is normal. Something in her eyes is off, as though she's shaken. An underlying crease of fright is apparent to Jess. "Cindy, is everything alright?" In an Eastern accent, "I know what your Grandmother sees and talks to is not real, but to her, it is, and at times it penetrates what I know to be real. During today, I don't know; it just didn't feel as though we were alone in the apartment." Cindy cuts herself off; as her tongue is getting carried away. She can see that she's frightening a young lady that already has far too much to deal with. "Never mind Jessica, I'm just getting old myself. I'll see you tomorrow night. Maybe I'll bring a friend, a good woman, to keep me company if that's okay?" "Of course, Cindy, I'll see you tomorrow, or you can stay for dinner." "I'll just go home, thank you."

Jessica hears her Grandmother talking the moment the door

closes. "I will eat all of my dinner Leonard, I promise...." a pause; "I'm glad she had a good day...." another pause; "I'll be sure not give her any trouble...." a long pause; "Yes, my friend, I'll be sure to tell her later." Jessica opens a can of tomato soup and turns on the stove to heat a frying pan for grilled cheese; her hairs rise. Cindy's right; it's as though they are not alone in the apartment. Grandma eats a whole grill cheese and has all of her soup; she also drinks two glasses of milk. They have a lovely night together, watching T.V. and cuddling on the couch. The older woman loses focus throughout the session. She looks around, sometimes staring blankly as though she hears something or asking about her Mother. Jessica assures her that her Mom is working. Unknown to Jessica, her Grandmother hears their voices and is well aware that her daughter has passed. In reality, she's feeling out Jess, seeing how she's coping; The Carneys have been keeping Irene fully updated.

Jessica has no problems putting her Grandmother to bed; she takes her pills, uses the toilet, and takes out her teeth on her own. Just after Jessica tucks her in, they share an extraordinary moment. Nan puts her cold hand on the teen's face; "You'll be alright, my dear, for you are powerful." Jessica hugs her Grandmother; she's crying softly, gently letting out the pain; "I love you, Nana."

True evil is bustling many floors below them; the black van has been reversed to the basement doors of the high rise. Shooter as he's called, the sergeant of arms of The Road Crew Mafia leads a couple of punks, expendables out the doors; they aren't worried about being seen. They take the four bound and gagged bangers from a different set out of the back of the truck. These young men are feeders as well, and they have no seniority within their pack; they're seen as servants to their colors. These boys will serve a purpose though, they may be disposable yet will be used in the art of negotiation by their leaders in the future; pawns lost in this dangerous sport. The unspoken King of this game watches from the parking lot. He's satisfied that his plan will bring closure to the inhabitants of Broken that crave private justice for what had taken place the night before. Uptown outsiders could never understand the laws of this nature, this graffiti-coded jungle. For he's the lion, the one that decides, the boogieman, the wizard behind the curtain. This devil only deals with Taylor and Malcolm Money Briggs, the two brothers that had shown the most promise. This killer placed them at the top of the food chain, and they've exceeded all expectations. Both follow instructions to the exact, without question. That's why this beast has laid in the weeds for so long now, his identity not known, as he's never directly involved in the wet work. The King knows that tomorrow all of the residents of Broken will see or hear about the four men that were found hanging in the court-yard, beaten, tortured, and burnt. They're the chosen sacrifices that had done the shooting, guilty or not; in the eyes of those in sorrow, they'll have paid the debt owing with blood.

Just as a straight razor is pulled deeply through the throat of the last victim in the basement to end the two hours of torture, Jessica suddenly awakes. She's in the dark and senses someone is close to her. Frightened, the teen reaches to her left and turns on her bedside lamp. Slowly her eyes begin to focus. She turns to her other side and lets out a scream! Nana is standing right beside her bed, with her grey hair hanging in her face as her arms are limp; it's as if something unseen is holding her up! Her eyes are open but pure white, as they are unnaturally turned up! "Are you okay, Grandma?" Jessica's voice is very shaky! Her Grandmother begins to whisper something; Jess can't make out what she's faintly chanting. As the startled teen gets up, she asks her Grandmother what she's saying. The limp older woman moves forward very quickly, seeming to float; the tone of her voice raises; it's different, demonic. "You know Jess, they either get Stitched or Kneaded," over and over, louder and louder, as her white eyes move back and forth! Jessica falls back on the bed; she's paralyzed with terror! The demonic voice is getting louder, and then she screams, "Jessica, Stitch is going to need your help!" The room is now dead silent as Nana falls into a limp heap onto the floor! It takes Jessica a few moments to regain her composure. She remembers and feels the words Molly Aiken had spoken to her earlier in the same chilling tone; "They either get Stiched or Kneaded." Grandma comes to as Jessica applies gentle touch; "Why am I on the floor, Jess?" "Are you hurt, Nana?" "I feel fine; I do have to pee, though." Her Grandmother stands up quickly, with some help, and they walk to the washroom; ten minutes later, she's peacefully sleeping. Jessica decides to relax on the couch. The movie on T.V. doesn't even register as background noise as the words spoken so demonically continue to cycle throughout her mind; "They either get Stitched or Kneaded." What does it mean? How could two women that do not know each other speak the exact words? Jessica Sworn's terror stems from the white eyes and that voice that seemed to shift between Molly Aiken and her Grandma. A tone of pure evil. "Stitch will need your help;" What does it mean? Jessica's eyelids finally surrender to what her body needs, for at this moment; there can be no answers.

What seems to be only a few minutes later, Jessica's woken up by the piercing sounds of emergency vehicles and their sirens violently rupturing the peaceful stillness of the apartment. The tired teen senses that she has woken later than usual; it's light outside. From her balcony, Jess sees the large crowd amassed in the courtyard. She looks at the four bodies that are bundled up, seeming to be in a group hug as they hang, swinging from the lamppost by a chain. Right then, her mind switches to the last image she'd seen in the dream she'd been having. Jessica can't remember the whole vision but senses it had terrified her. The most vivid memory had been the cat in room sixty-seven at the nursing home, with its creepy marble eyes! That wretched furry statue that Molly Aiken seemed to be hypnotized by.

Cynthia shows up at eight, accompanied by a friend named Ira; fifteen minutes later, they're both having vodka and orange juices at the kitchen table. Her Grandmother had gone to bed without any trouble, saying she was tired from watching her new program on the blank television. Her Nan had no memory of what had happened the night before.

When Jess arrives at the home early, she finds her three co-workers at the nurse's station, quick introductions are made. The registered nurse is Karen; she's a tired-looking woman that seems too small to be holding the massive canister of coffee she drinks from. The other two are nurse's-aides, named Mark and Jennifer. The male orderly is a big man, seeming huge as he sits beside Karen. He smiles a lot and is friendly, welcoming Jessica to the graveyard shift, telling her that he liked her Mother. Jennifer is young and in excellent shape. She also compliments Jessica's Mother while giving condolences. Jessica remembers seeing all of them at the wake; they looked different, though, as they'd all been in their street clothes. Karen, sensing the teen's sadness, turns the staff's attention to the day and afternoon reports. The main focus is a new admit; a man named Arthur Smith. The three experienced nurses are happy to find out that Arthur is continent and very friendly.

Jessica centers herself, leaving the strange events of the last night alone, turning her attention to her duties on the floor. She follows Lynn's instructions, taking her time and doing it right. During the first few hours, other than one of her co-workers getting up to answer the odd call bell, the teen's alone with her work. Just as Jessica is about to empty a wastebasket, she senses someone coming down the hall. Molly Aiken walks past her with her head down; her long scraggly white hair hides her face, yet Jessica knows it's her. The older woman's arms are stretched out from her sides. It's as though each of her hands is being held by someone else. A very foul smell of rot accompanies the older woman as she passes by. Jessica is about to say something but freezes; she senses another presence in the dark corridor and decides to follow Molly at a distance. As she proceeds, Jessica hears her Nan's demonic voice repeating the phrase, "They either get Stitched or Kneaded," within her head...Molly disappears around a corner. Jessica peaks around the bend, and the sleep-walker has stopped in front of another resident's door. Molly's arms suddenly drop to her sides, limp, as though she's let go of the invisible hands. After standing there for about a minute, the old lady methodically turns towards Jessica and slowly walks again. Frightened, Jess heads for the nurse's station; there's nobody there! Quickly she runs towards room sixty-seven. Just as Jess enters the hall, Molly is going back into her room.

Jessica heads back to the nurse's station. Again it is empty; she decides to wait. Jess is very nervous; she doesn't know her new co-workers and is scared they won't believe her and that they'll probably think she's crazy and laugh behind her back. Lynn had made it very clear to Jessica that she's an extra set of eyes for the nursing staff and that she must report anything she sees out of the ordinary. After a few minutes that seem to take forever, the others come down another hall together. Jessica summons her courage, "I just saw Molly Aiken sleepwalking;" there is no laughter. "Did you wake her up;" Karen asks? "I, no, I was shocked, I guess." "Whose door did she stop in front of Jessica;" Mark asks? "I'm not sure; I can show you though, why?"

Karen gets the vitals machine, and Jessica leads them to the room; it belongs to the new admit Arthur Smith. The three nurses go in and turn the lights on. "Hello Arthur, my name is Karen; I'm the charge nurse. I'm just here to check your vitals." The older man doesn't reply. Jessica moves closer to the bed and watches; the elderly resident doesn't appear to be breathing and is very still. Arthur's mouth is stretched wide open as though he's trying to scream. His eyes are wide open with an expression of terror; his blue pupils are glazed over. Karen checks for a pulse; "I'm not getting anything guys, I'm afraid he's expired." "You're not going to perform C.P.R Karen?" "He was a D.N.R. Jessica, it means no resuscitation," Karen then instructs Mark and Jennifer to accompany Jessica to Molly's room. "Better bring your cleaning supplies, Jessica." "Why?" the shaken teen asks? "This has happened before, and Molly is always sick right after." "What happens?" "Exactly what just took place, Jessica, the same situation. Molly had sleepwalked to another resident's room and stood outside of it for a few minutes. A few hours later, we found that resident expired, and soon after, we found Molly sitting on the edge of her bed; there was vomit everywhere." "Hopefully, for your sake, youngster, not everything will be the same," Mark kids.

"Don't be a jerk, Mark, okay; this isn't funny, especially for someone who's working their first shift." "You're right, Jen, sorry Jess, I'll help you out any way I can."

Jessica has to stop before going into the room; she leans against her cleaning cart as the smell of acidy vomit overwhelms her nasal. Just as advertised, there's puke everywhere! Molly sits on the edge of her bed, staring at the stuffed cat. A call bell goes off. The sound cuts through the room; it's different from the others that Jessica has heard throughout the night. "That's a tag alarm, Jess. We both have to check on that one; there may have been a fall. Why don't you wait in the hall until we're back." Jessica nods and follows the two PSW's out of the room.

Molly watches the shadow of Stitch slither across the wall as though it's following the young girl; she waits a minute. When she's sure the others are gone, she speaks, "Why don't you come in here dear, keep an old lady company. My cat seems to like you." Jessica's nerves electrify as she feels everything around her go still. "I'm just a little old lady; I won't bite you. Besides, my teeth aren't in." Jess will do as she's told and wait for Mark and Jennifer to come back. She jumps when she feels the hand on her shoulder; she turns to see Molly Aiken in the door. "Come in and help me clean this mess;" Jessica is shaking! "I didn't mean to scare you, dear; today has been a big day for me. Something I've been pursuing for years is almost finished. Give me a facecloth and a towel; let's help out your co-workers and make you look good at the same time." Jessica hesitates for a minute; she doesn't want to upset the older woman. However, workers in the home do not perform tasks outside of their scope of practice. Broken hips kill a very high percentage of older people, and she's worried Molly could fall. Mostly she's frightened by the older woman's energy.

"Please, dear, I'm quite embarrassed." Jessica takes some clothes off the cart and motions for Molly to lead her into the fouled room. "My other nightgowns are in that drawer, dear." Jess is so nervous once the bathroom door shuts. She feels terrible for the elder, though, as age has wrinkled and bruised her skin; the older woman's flesh is almost translucent. Jessica spots vomit on Mollies back, and instinct takes over. She wets a face-cloth with warm water and begins gently cleaning the fragile epidermis. The teen knows what she's doing, as she's been help-ing her Grandmother for years. Quickly it becomes evident that Molly is much more capable than expected.

Mark and Jennifer return to the room, both dreading the horrible task that lies ahead; "Where are they, Mark?" The large man looks at his work partner and shrugs. They both hear voices coming from the washroom; they quietly approach the door. They can't hear what's being said, but surprisingly Molly is en-gaged in conversation with the new housekeeper. Mark motions with his head for Jennifer to go and get Karen. More than once, a resistive resident has opened up to a new staff member; how-ever, this seems impossible in Molly Aiken's case. The charge nurse has just called the family of the deceased and the funeral home that's to take care of Arthur Sander's body. "Karen, Jessica's in the washroom with Molly, apparently helping her." "How so; you two shouldn't have left her alone with her." "A tag alarm went off, and we told her to wait in the hall until we returned. They're having a full-out conversation." Karen is one of the staff that has consistently argued that Molly is catatonic. Her very sel-dom words are nothing more than confusion, stemming from a sudden surge of long-term memory. Curiosity compels her not to start the charting that will take up a good deal of her night. The highly qualified and experienced nurse shakes her head at the two P.S.W.'s in disbelief as she listens to the banter that's going on the other side of the door. Karen asks that her co-workers do not clean the room and directs them out in the hall. Dealing with Molly Aiken when she decides not to comply is be-yond stressful. A P.S.W. that's now on stress leave had followed Molly back to her room as she'd slept-walked, trying to wake her, gently putting her hands on the resident. The gentle persuasion had to have continued into the room. When Mark had found his former work partner, she'd been lying in a puddle of blood from a head wound, completely unconscious.

Karen knocks on the door, and against her better judgment, opens it up; the curiosity is too compelling. Molly's chattering away. She stops as she locks eyes with the charge nurse; her head drops to the floor. A less experienced nurse would pry; Karen nods at Jessica and closes the door. "I don't want this interaction stopped. Mark, you wait in the hall and be ready to intervene if the situation escalates. I will help Jennifer prepare Mr. Sander's corpse for transportation." A few minutes later, Mark hears the washroom door open. He can't make out what is being said, but the tone of the conversation suggests that Molly is content. "I'll be right back to clean your room, Molly." Jessica feels an overwhelming sense of pride as she exits Molly's room, as though she'd accomplished a task others haven't been able to. "Good job Jessica. However, this being said, please don't go into a room if I ask you not to. It's for your safety." Mark isn't jealous of the new girl's ability to deal with a resident that has resisted him. Nor is his ego bruised by the new girls' disobedience; he just wants his co-workers to be safe. The image of Meagan out cold and bloody haunts this good man. "Sorry, Mark I...." "Enough said, Jess, good job. Jennifer and I were going to clean the room. We didn't want to interrupt the positive interaction you were having with Molly. Jen and I appreciate what you just did." "You want me to continue then, Mark?" "Go for it. I'll be right out here in case the situation deteriorates."

Jessica thanks Mark and pushes the cleaning cart into room sixty-seven. Molly sits in the chair, holding the stuffed cat; "This is Stitch Jessica; it's been my companion for a very long time." As Jess begins setting up to deep clean the room, she feels like she's being watched. As she commences, the teen periodically looks towards the cat; its piercing marbled gaze is always upon her. Jessica's senses pick up more, though, as if there's an unseen presence in the room, a definite feeling that she and Miss. Aiken are not alone. Jessica feels that honesty is the only way to maintain this unexpected relationship and conveys her feelings to the creepy resident. "Stitch scares me, Molly, I looked into its eyes yesterday, and now they're ingratiated into my being. I saw them in a nightmare I had last night." "You can't run from things that won't let you Jessica, your Grandmother knows all about that." Jessica had told Molly about her Grandmother while helping her in the washroom, but her words had been vague. Mollie's reply suggests familiarity with her Nan; "How so Molly?" "In time, Jessica, all will be revealed to you." While Jessica cleans, they talk. She promises Molly she will bring her a coffee from Martin's the next night, apparently her favorite brand. As youth carefully disinfects the room, the bond between them strengthens, all the while the shadow of Stitch dancing on the wall, always behind Jessica, watching, listening, and craving.

Arthur Smith wasn't the last one left that had been in the barn that night, cheering, as The Brothers were shown to the darkness; there's still one more that begs to be cleansed of the atrocity that had scarred his soul. Arthur's corpse is loaded into the back of the Hurst, but his consciousness is in a much darker place. It's with the shadows who seek redemption through the unnatural manipulation of his supernatural soul.

Chapter 4

The Charge nurse had been happy to let Jessica sit with Molly for the next few hours that night; she and the other two had taken turns sitting outside of the door, keeping watch. Jessica had found herself entranced by Molly's life as a Carney; the older woman had told one fascinating story after another about her gypsy life. Molly had left out any details surrounding the supernatural. The older woman had eventually told Jess she was ready to sleep, and soon after the teen left the room, she'd done so, for the rest of the shift, without interruption. The three nurses had been very grateful to Jess, each thanking her for redirecting what could have been a time-consuming drama. Jessica had gone on to quickly finishing her housekeeping duties before the end of the shift. Upon getting back to broken pavement, Jessica had run into Detective Smith, who was with a couple of uniforms in the elevator. "Let me guess, young lady, you didn't hear anything or see anything?" "Just the four bodies hanging in the courtyard." The detective had stared at her hard; an artery beside his right eye had seemed close to exploding. "Theirs a lot of people that can't see or hear living in this building, young lady." "It's a much safer existence." "Keep living that way, and we'll see how safe it is," the detective had loudly replied. Cynthia had been pretty cut in the morning; the vodka was almost finished. Ira was passed out on the couch. "Your grandmother slept all night; we had no trouble with her at all." It had taken Cindy a few minutes to wake up Ira, and they left. After a couple of hours of watching T.V., her Grandmother had awakened. She took her pills and had breakfast without resistance. Jessica had slept all day. When she'd awoken and quickly gone to the living room, she'd found Nana sitting in her chair, staring at the white fuzz on the television. She'd been laughing; "I love this program, Jessica; I love the life of a Carney so." Jessica's mind craved to investigate the strange parallel of Carney's life between her Grandmother and Molly Aiken. The overwhelmed teen left it alone, chalking it up to a strange coincidence. This is the routine she quickly greases into over the next few months. As promised, she'd picked up a coffee from Martin's, and after she'd been done her duties, knocked on Mollie's door, who'd been sitting on the edge of her bed starring at Stitch. Molly had been catatonic throughout the day. The other two shifts had found it almost impossible to believe what they'd heard in report about the resident's behavior with Jessica. The instant Jessica had entered the room, it was as though a switch flipped on, and Molly began conversing with the teenager. On that same night, Martha watched the video of Jessica and Mollie's exchange with a friend, which specializes in the science of sleep. The footage had been captured on a tiny camera strategically placed so that it couldn't be seen. Yet, the image was of the entire room. The picture had clipped in and out with intense flashes of light. Over the next few months, Martha and her friend meet five nights a week to watch the hidden footage of Molly Aiken. It's their obsession, watching the older woman sit catatonic all day, and then as though a switch flips, come to life when Jessica enters the room each night. Martha goes out of her way to encourage the teen to continue her late-night visits. Unknown to Martha, her friend takes the footage to a colleague who specializes in manipulating video. Images of the supernatural are frame frozen, ranging from skulls of a cat to those of humans. This lady's obsession with proving a theory has jaded her to a fault, and lying comes with the territory. Each night, the shadow of Stitch marinates the wall behind the teen. The giant shadow purring away, nudging its darkness against Jessica. Molly knows she's close to the abyss, as she's always cold; she feels her cells close to shutting down. Molly Aiken knows she's found the new owner for Stitch. Still, her morals prevent her from handing this tortured life of supernatural occult over to this young, innocent girl. Jessica says goodbye to Cynthia and Ira every night, besides her one night off; they're always on time, and there hasn't been one problem with the routine. Every morning it's the same, as though robotic, Cynthia is finishing the vodka, Ira is passed out on the couch. Granny takes her pills as usual and sits in her chair, staring at the white fuzz on the television, quickly becoming engaged with what only she can see. Jessica sleeps well, as she's content with this new life. The charge nurse on the day shift is shocked when she sees Molly Aiken's room number light up on the call bell sign. Two nurse's aids go to find out if Molly accidentally rang the bell or if the creepy old lady actually needs help. Both workers are nervous as they approach the room. The two women are surprised to find Molly sitting on the edge of her bed; she's wearing a black dress that would have been very chic decades before. "Can we do something for you, Molly?" "I will need a pen and a paper;" the hauntingly deep and high voice causes' their skin to crawl. "For what, Molly?" The resident doesn't take her eyes from the marbles of Stitch; she's made her decision, as she's tired of waiting for them to show her the darkness. "That would be my business, ladies. Is there something a law against an old lady wanting to write something down?" "Of course not Molly, I'll be right back." Martha, who had just gotten the call from the charge nurse, moves quickly to observe the interaction firsthand. The Director of Care wants to hear what's being said. By the time she gets to the room, Molly's signing her name to a document. "Get that pen away from her now," The DOC screams! Molly turns to her, "I know you and your friend have been watching me, Martha!" There's an uncomfortable pause, dead air. Then very methodically, the old lady drives the pen into her neck, over and over again! The nurses do everything in their power to save Molly, but she crosses over quickly. This devout practitioner of the occult is welcomed with hollow bones into the darkness.

Strangely enough, just as the charge nurse is looking for Molly's contact number, a man dressed in a black suit, and a cloak, shows up, asking for her. His eyes are large and brown; another man, a hazardous-looking type, accompanies him. They both appear to be from a different time, dressed in vintage clothing that suggests the work of a skilled tailor. Martha had read the note left by Molly, instructing that the few things she has are to be thrown out, except for the stuffed cat, that is to go to Jessica. Martha has planned on taking the cat for herself. Usually, in a case like Molly's, most of her items would end up in the trash. Martha isn't a thief and sees no harm in taking the cat if no one else claims it, but this last-minute will has created a moral issue. This good woman ponders the decision and decides that Jessica isn't supposed to accept gifts from residents and that the animal will come with her. There's a knock at her door! Martha suddenly feels as though she's been caught shoplifting, as though whoever's at the door knows the dirty little secret she's about to forge. "Martha, I presume," the DOC feels time stop, as the stranger walks into the room. "I see you have Stitch with you?" "Who's Stitch?" "Molly's cat, I've spoken to the other girls already; apparently, Molly had just written and signed a letter. I would like to see it." "Who are you? No, may I see some I.D. please, sir?" There's an air about the strange visitor, his complete style and look as if he's traveled through time. "I'm well aware of your interest in that cat Martha; however, that's not your property. You do an outstanding job here at the home, and that is why I'm going to disregard your intentions with that property." The visitor has Martha's full attention; she's at a loss for words, as she's just been accused of theft, and as minor as the infraction may seem, it's true. The handsome young man then shows Martha his license. After being instructed to look up specific facts on her computer, she's shocked. "The cat will go to Jessica, Sir." "Its name is Stitch;" with a quick turn and a snap of his cloak, the powerful young man is gone. Jessica's surprised when she sees a police cruiser outside of the home. Martha comes out of her office; "Jess, I need to talk to you, please;" the teenager is scared she's done something wrong. "Am I in trouble?" "No, no, not at all, Jess; you're doing a fantastic job." Her relief only lasts for a second as she sees Molly's cat sitting on Martha's desk. "Why is Stitch in here, Martha?" The director takes a moment; everyone in this field takes losing a resident differently. "That is why I stayed here tonight Jess, what I need to talk to you about; Molly took her own life earlier today by stabbing herself in the neck with a pen." "What, oh my, that is just terrible!" The tears immediately stream from her eyes. "She asked for the pen; she was supervised. We didn't even know she could write." "What did she write?" "This is just it; she made a final testament that she wanted you to have Stitch. We were going to throw the cat away, but we know how close you had gotten with Molly over the past few months. The relationship you developed with her was truly remarkable, Jessica." She can feel the marble eyes on her. Jessica isn't even sure she wants Stitch. It just scares her, but she'd become close to Molly. This older woman was the person that she'd spoken the most with since her mother had died. The image of Molly writing the note for her and then pushing the pen through her withered flesh brings about more crying. "I would love to respect her final wishes Martha; I will give Stitch a good home." "I know the broad strokes of your job Jessica, and I feel it would be better for you to take a sick day for this shift. Molly took her own life, and the police have been upstairs investigating. Her room is roped off; however, Molly's body, her blood, is still there. We're not able to release her corpse until they're finished." "It's my job, Martha." The nurse thinks back to the conversation she'd had earlier with the stranger. "I'll take care of this Jess, go home and rest, please." Jessica can feel the eyes upon her as she sits on the bus holding Stitch. She smells the odor that has always accompanied the cat, but in the large room hadn't been so strong. Jess had made a point of never getting close to it before. It isn't the stench of rotting flesh as one might think; it's strange, a hint of dying flowers, withering poppies marinated in sprinkles of aged epidermis. Jessica thinks of Molly and some of the stories she'd told, of her life as a Carney. She was a fascinating woman, and the teen will miss her; she'd grown quite fond of their late-night visits. As usual, there's been some sort of drama at Broken Pavement. Soldiers of The Road Crew Mafia are mouthing off to the police; none of their pants cover their bums. They're all wearing expensive clothing, and none of them seem to be able to speak without using obscenities. "As we told you, pig, we don't know no cat named Gerald Fold, so go tug some else's junk!" Jessica slides unnoticed past the small crowd; thankfully, the police are there. She'd been worried about someone taking Stitch from her on the way to the apartment. "Jessica, you're here, and what is that thing you're carrying." Cindy is delighted, so is Ira. The vodka has taken effect." "It's a long story." "Sit down with us girls and have a drink; tell us all about it. I know you're young, but you look old enough to buy the vodka, so have a drink." "I'll have some orange juice and tell you about it, Cindy. I don't intend on ever drinking alcohol or taking drugs in my life; certainly, you understand?" The older woman gets the point. "Of course, my dear, I know what you mean and respect that very much." Cindy points for Jessica to take a seat; she does and puts Stitch on the table. Cindy goes to the kitchen and gets a glass of orange juice; Ira can smell the strange aroma and feels her skin crawl as she stares into the marbled soul of the dead cat. Although Jessica knows she's never to speak names of the residents or information about their lives, she tells the older women about the strange relationship she'd had with Molly Aiken. The teen doesn't mention her name. Jessica cries as she recants the peculiar journey that had ended with the resident's self-mutilation with a pen. "I would cherish this dead cat, Jessica. It's a momentum of you doing an outstanding job," Cindy comments. Although Ira agrees out loud, inside, she wants to get away from the eerie trophy as she senses an evil presence surrounding it. The company is suitable for Jessica. It grounds her, temporarily creating an illusion that she's living everyday life, but too soon, it's over. The older women take normality and the vodka with them. The teen checks on Nana, who seems to be having a nightmare; Jessica gently wakes her up, intending to take her to the bathroom. "Oh Jessica, I never should have done it. I have brought nothing but bad fortunes to my family, to my daughter, and you!" "Grandma, it's okay let's go to the bathroom." "I don't need to go to the bathroom, I need to go with them, and I need to pay for what I did to them!" Her Grandmother's strength is surreal, and Jessica knows she would have to physically hurt her if she's going to get her to move from the bed, and so she walks away. After a few minutes outside of the room, the sound of crying stops; Jessica gets ready for bed. On her way, Jessica spots the small side table her mother used to use for smoking; perfect, she thinks, and takes it to her room. She places it in the right corner, opposite her bed. Just as she thought, Stitch looks perfect on it, and she feels Molly's presence in the room. As she gets comfortable in bed, the teen senses those marble eyes upon her, and she pretends as though an angel watches over her in the dark, and soon a gentle sleep washes throughout. Jessica suddenly wakes up and immediately feels a gentle rubbing against her feet. She tries to get up and look, but she can't move. An acute static electric surge is felt, stinging her nerves as though a car battery is manipulating her central nervous system. With all of her strength, she tries to move, nothing, and she feels her heart rate speeding up. The gentle brushing turns into a feeling of tiny feet walking up her legs; she feels them gently passing over her flesh. Jessica tries to let a scream out of her mouth that she can tell is stretched wide open. Now she sees the Shadow of a cat upon her chest; its eyes are glowing red! The animal's weight is on her, its paws gently kneading her breasts, harder and harder; inside her, the energy of the electrical current is too much. Jessica, desperate to get a breath, summons every bit of will she has to survive as she stares into the glowing red eyes. Then she feels a powerful internal pop! Jessica is now looking down on her own body, which is paralyzed in bed. She's not breathing. Her head is raised as though her chin is being pushed into her chest. The ridged position of her body is very unnatural. Seeing her eyes and mouth so stretched as the shadow of the red-eyed animal kneads her chest makes her want to feel terror; she doesn't. Jessica looks at herself in the standing form; she isn't whole but ghostly, for she's her spirit, a substance of pure consciousness. The cat's silhouette jumps from the bed. She feels it going through her legs gently. It then goes to the wall; its shadow grows large, and she follows it to the left corner of the room. Three dark figures are standing there, two small and one very large. They stand with their backs to her. They all turn towards her in sequence; she wants to feel terrified as they also have glowing red eyes. She looks at her body on the bed; she wants it to wake up and move to run. The shadow of the cat then jumps into the arms of the huge shadow man, and they advance in sequence towards her. Jess wills her spirit to move, to the right, as do the three visitors; she feels trapped. The smaller ones raise their hands. The motion isn't threatening; she thinks of Molly at this moment, what she may have been seeing, the sleepwalking that night. There's a strong smell of rotting meat, death, as the Shadowmen are upon her. The two little shadows each take one of her hands; the sense of touch is gentle, friendly. The hands are large, and so are their heads; she senses that they are Dwarfs. Jessica feels a mass of energy touch her shoulder. It's the hand of the towering shadow; although it's icy, it calms her, its touch suggests protection. Suddenly she feels a surge, a current. Jessica can no longer see; she just feels their collective energy move as one floating mass, together. A few moments later, they stop; she senses they are still in the apartment. There's another surge, a stronger current, and everything goes black. Irene feels her legs twitch. There's a burning sensation going through her core, again the twitching; suddenly, she feels as though there's sand being dumped onto her chest. The older woman's still in a state of light sleep. The elder commands her brain to deliver a message to wake up, to move, nothing! A hideous foul odor is evident. The Shadow of Stitch jumps onto her chest. Its claws strike the flesh, but the shadow is careful not to go too deep; she fully awakes. Irene knows her time has finally come, as she feels their hands grip her wrists and ankles. She's waited for the three shadows to come. To exact the deserving vengeance upon her since that night of chaos in the barn. The grips of the shadow men aren't painful but firm as to hold her place. The tremendous weight on her chest is without mercy. It's as if seven wheelbarrows full of sand have been dumped on her at once! Her old heart kicks into overdrive as it tries to deliver oxygen to her blood. This is the moment Irene is finally able to force her eyes open. The black cat that sits on her chest is the size of a tiger. Its eyes glow red; she cannot move, nor can she breathe properly, only just enough. Irene can feel her mouth stretching wide open; she can barely see to her sides. It's the small ones holding her wrists, the Dwarfs. The big Shadow has her legs; he's doing so with only one hand. Irene tries to scream, as she feels a very sharp prick in her left toe, and then another, and another! She feels the supernatural thread going through her foot with each stab and pull, it hurts, and then she remembers, "They either get Stitched or Kneaded. Irene can not scream, she can not move, all she has is her senses and sight; she will allow herself to be taken into the darkness with dignity. As her feet and hands are stitched to the bed, the older woman feels a sense of relief; she'd been raised by good god-fearing country folk. Since that night she'd helped lure these brothers into the woods, and to the barn, where Carl Hester exacted what he called private justice, this good woman has always lived with guilt and fear. With every supernatural Stitch she feels attaching her flesh to the mattress, theirs a sense of her soul being cleansed. The Shadow-Brothers are not aggressive about their work. There's a sense of having to do something that needs to be done as if they're not taking pleasure in this haunting task of the occult. The pain burns in her old hands and feet; although it has seemed to have taken at least an hour, it's only been a few minutes. As the right hand is almost sewn to the bed, Irene suddenly hears music. The type she remembers hearing when she was young, a child while holding her parent's hands at a carnival. Many happy people have listened to this music while forgetting about their problems as they ride the merry-go-round. Then there's a bright light in the room. Stitch forces its supernatural energy harder and harder on her chest! Irene feels her body being pushed deep into the mattress. The integrity of the supernatural Stitch is being tested. Just as her innards feel like they'll be vomited out of her stretched mouth and sprayed throughout the room, she feels a booming pop throughout her body. The large cat lets out a screech as it jumps from her chest! Irene feels like she's now standing and looks down; she sees her ridged body stitched to the bed. One of the Dwarfs stands beside her; the other is across from her. The large one stands at the foot of her bed, holding the now domestic-sized shadow cat. She feels her hand being taken; its eyes glow as it wraps the cold energy around her fingers. The light and music come from a tunnel that's appeared on the wall. There's a mouth around the tunnel. Brown disgusting mis-shaped teeth edge the supernatural passage. The lips are small and dirty, Irene recognizes the mouth; Carl Hester's grin was infamous throughout Green-bud, even before what happened to them in his gruesome death. Irene feels a pull. She complies and follows the shadowy grip; she only wishes she could say goodbye to Jessica before entering the tunnel. The light gets brighter and brighter as they walk, the music louder and louder, but for her, theirs only laughing during her crossing through this paranormal passage. Soon these spirits come through the light; their bodies take form. They are at a Carnival, and its day time. The gypsies are together, laughing, and talking; they're having a group lunch. Irene watches a handsome man dressed in a cloak serving the others; he appears to be their leader. This man is gracious and does not put on an air that he's better than the ones that work for him. The Count looks towards Irene and the Brother's; he waves to them, welcoming them to come to join the meal. The Brothers are still touching Irene; they've never been angry with her, and over the past few months, have tried to convey a sense of friendliness through the white fuzz. As Jessica was brought closer and closer to the occult that's permanently shadowed her, making this old soul comfortable has been the shadow's primary concern. Only wanting to end the sorrow of that darkest of nights. Unlike the others who had so savagely taken The Brothers' lives and brought such sorrow onto the

Never Sleep Swing Company, Irene Sworn had tried to warn the Brothers. She'd lived her life with tremendous guilt, and this is why she only needs to apologize to this tight-knit group of humans. To tell them all before they enjoy lunch together in this different plane of existence; how sorry she has always been. How she's always wished she's warned them about Carl Hester's horrible plan before leaving the Carnival grounds. The clan welcomes her apology with open arms and accepts Irene as one of their own.

Chapter 5

J essica feels an intense sensation of having to pee as she slowly feels her being coming to. The teen opens her eyes and feels turned around. Jess realizes she's at the wrong end of her bed. Through the fogged gaze of unfocused eyes, she's met by the piercing glare of Stitch. Slowly she sits up; that's strange, she thinks to herself. The light coming in from the window is bright; what time is it, she wonders? Jessica looks at her clock 12:01 pm; "Nana," she shouts as she rushes from her bed! Jess almost falls as she steps in something very slippery; "Gross," she says aloud as she realizes it's vomit. Jessica's mind quickly hypothesizes that Nana was in her room the night before and had gotten sick. Jess hops on one leg while using her hands to grab things to keep her balance on her way to the closet. The teen takes an old T-shirt out and wipes her foot off. Before leaving the room, she drops the shirt onto the dark puddle of vomit. Jessica listens for her Grandma, nothing. She assumes she's on the couch staring at the television; she quickly gets to the toilet and relieves herself.

As Jessica brushes her teeth, she feels a slight sense of pain as her nightshirt rubs on the flesh of her chest. She pulls her shirt down and finds many tiny scratches; they're barely visible. Jess looks at her fingernails; she'd just cut them. They're not sharp at all; strange, she thinks to herself. As she brushes her teeth, she gets a feeling she'd dreamt, and she pulls the shirt down again. No memory forms in her mind, just a heightening sense that something had taken place while sleeping. Grandma isn't on the couch; she hurries to her room, "Nana," she shouts and rushes to her bedside! Jessica's loving touch is met with Rigor Mortis; she falls to her knees crying. Jess wants to hug her Grandmother, but that ice-cold stiffness of death prevents her from doing so. Nana's once bright eyes are glazed over, the smell of poop is very evident. A blackened fluid has run from her nose, but it's the expression on her Grandmother's face that assures the devastated teen that she'll lose sleep thinking about this horrible moment. It's the way Nana's mouth is stretched so wide open, so stiff, as if there's a hidden device in her mouth that's prying her jaw past the point of extension. Jessica places her hands on her Grandma's head and chin; the icy flesh, dead to touch, causes her almost to be sick, and as she tries to close the stiff jaw, she feels a crack and vomits into her mouth. Jess sits by the bed for quite some time crying, unable to touch the woman that had always watched her when she was a young child. Nana was the person she'd known the most, that had known her the most; she feels very guilty for not be able to give her gentle touch. Nan's body stretched out while her head is pushed into her chest, and her legs raised, so stiff, looks as though she'd been fighting to breathe.

Jess decides to move towards what her Mother had told her to do in case of sudden death; she can hear her Mother's voice; "We don't need the extra charges of the ambulance, hospital, and of course dialing the emergency response number Jess." How right her Mother had been, as the way her death had been handled through the hospital had taken a nice bite out of the tiny nest egg the nursing home had given Jess. "Just dial this number and give this case number to whoever asks for it at the funeral home; it's all paid for, Jess. Remember, call me first, so I can get home to be with you." How badly the shaken sixteen-year-old wishes her Mother was with her right now. Jessica wants to clean her Grandmother up, take the soiled clothing and bedding away from her body, but she can't even bring herself to go back into the room. Over the past few months, Jessica had deep cleaned four rooms of residents that had expired, while the corpses had still been present. Their faces had looked at peace, and The Nurses Aids had washed and dressed the bodies. Although Jess could have easily done what they'd done by the fourth death, she can't deal with her Nan, as she doesn't want to look at her, as she appears to be in a frozen state of lonely terror. Jessica's ashamed, and never as much as when she watches the morticians wheel her Grandmother on the gurney out of the apartment, as she's all alone in that body bag, so stiff and dirty. "Let me know when I can pick up her ashes, please. I don't ever want to see her like that again." The man's feeble attempt to console her by telling her it's natural to feel this way does nothing for her. Jessica feels that her Mother would be so disappointed in her if she's watching at this moment.

Martha's suddenly awoken from a deep sleep she's having in her office after doing her best to clean the home the night before. The DOC had spent a good portion of her time in Molly's room. Every cleaning movement had helped repair her shamed soul. Martha's entire being has been marinated with guilt since the young stranger had called her out on her malfeasants involving Molly Aiken. The look in those brown eyes, his conviction, the way her world had turned upside down when he provided proof of who he was. "Jessica's on the phone, Martha, line one." Martha centers herself before going to her desk and picking up the phone. The moment Jessica hears Martha's voice, she breaks down, and as she cries hard, she assures her boss, she'll be in for her shift later that night. Martha decides that she'll go to the apartment and ask Lynn to come with her. "Lynn and I are coming now. If you can, will you meet us in the front foyer?" This offer calms her; however, Jess feels the foyer isn't safe for them. "I'll meet you in the plaza just up from Broken, Martha; it's much safer there." "Are you sure, Jess?" "I want out of here now, there's a smell Martha, and I just can't bring myself to clean her room." "I understand, Jess."

Forty minutes later, Lynn and Martha envelop their beings around their friend's daughter. They both know this young lady's been through way too much. They go into a diner, and it's quickly decided over coffees that Lynn and Martha will clean Nana's room. "Also, Jess, you have sick days accumulated. You're not coming into work for at least a week, and if need be, I'll stay with you." After trying to convince her boss that work will keep her from thinking of her Nan, resting alone in the body bag, Jessica agrees. Lynn feels she's going to have a panic attack as they cross through the courtyard of the housing project. The frightened woman can feel the evil surrounding her as her eyes pick up so much illegal on their way to the elevator. Catcalls are delivered to the three women throughout their journey through the gator pond concentrated by gang-banging degenerates.

Cindy's just gotten rid of a garbage bag and greets them in the hall. Upon hearing the news of Irene's sudden death, this hardened woman genuinely hugs Laura's daughter. She's unable to hide her tears from the two strangers. Cindy wants to help and meets them back at the apartment with a new bottle of vodka and some orange juice; the three older women each take a stiff drink, Jess passes on the liquor. "Why does it smell so badly;" she continues to ask her friends as they clean the apartment top to bottom? None of them can taste the occult darkness that has so invasively entered Jessica's life. Martha feels drawn towards Stitch throughout the day. Still, she keeps her word to the powerful young man in her office, leaving her obsessions and curiosities to be researched far away from Jessica Sworn. Lynn takes Cindy's advice at five pm; if she's not spending the night, now's the time to get a cab. Soon the true vampires of Broken Pavement will awake from their drug-induced slumbers, as the blanket of the night is their signal to search for blood. They go together, meeting the cab at the plaza. Jessica, Cindy, and Martha make it back to the apartment without incident. Cindy says goodnight near the end of their second bottle of vodka. The apartment appears to be clean, but their's is a darkness attached to the scent that the teen still smells. Jessica thanks her for everything and gives her older friend a good hug before she leaves.

Jess returns to the table; Martha's very drunk. "This isn't very appropriate, Jessica; I don't drink like this ever. Please keep this between us, and don't mention it to any of our co-workers." Martha then gets up from the table and manages to make her way to the washroom; Jess finds her passed out on the toilet twenty minutes later. It's a struggle arousing Martha from her drunken slumber, but eventually, Jessica's able to get her boss to the couch. The older woman refuses a glass of water, assuring Jess she's fine and is soon snoring very loud. After a half-hour of watching her friend and determining her boss would be alright, Jessica heads to bed; she's exhausted. Never has she felt this emotionally spent. As she passes her Grandmother's room, her eyes swell up again; she can still smell the rot. The other ladies had all agreed they hadn't smelt it in the first place. Even with all the emotional cleansing done, Jessica's entire being is still very aware of the foul. Although the funk lies below the typical odor, it's there, and it's intense. The teen doesn't bother to turn the lights on in her room, nor does she set her alarm. For a moment, she stares at the shadow of her dead pet. She imagines its marble eyes and feels a strong sense of DeJaVu, a strong impulse of recognition, but she can't place it. The feeling is not of Molly Aiken; it's a spike of recognition, a hint of a past life; she loses the sense as fast as it had come. As if the silhouette of her bed is inviting her fatigue, she goes to it. Jess falls on top of the mattress; it's as though she travels right through it and lands on sleep.

Not much later, her senses feel the fur of the shadow cat lovingly brushing against her toes. Soon Stitch is kneading the conduit; it watches the human's eyes open, and immediate fear registers. The entity tries to convey gentle; before applying the weight needed to draw out the human's spirit. As the kneading intensifies precisely to what is required, Jessica finds it harder to breathe, and just as panic sets in; her mouth opens wide, so desperate to survive. The burning inside her lungs peaks, and then comes the loud internal pop of the release. The shadow hops from the vessel's chest and begins rubbing itself on the apparition that's now beside the bed. Jessica's subconscious watches the three Shadowmen turn in sequence from the opposite corner, their eyes glowing red. Stitch meets them as they come to her, hopping into the arms of the one who saved it and gives it love. Jessica's spirit is still as she takes the cold touch of the small visitors. Their dark energy forms around innocence. As the contrasting supernatural currents melt into one, the spiritual orb begins to float. They sense the human on the couch as they pass over; but pay this one no attention, for she's not part of their hunt. Humans in the orb's path may feel the sudden dropping in temperature or the smell of rot. A curious young child that watches their surroundings closely might see a ripple in their vision, giving sight to a ghostly limb or face. Still, the few humans that do pass by are not in touch with this sense, their souls lost, as they focus on acquiring substance. The Shadowmen go where Jessica's subconscious leads them, as though she's a paranormal G.P.S. How Jessica managed to remain so innocent in the presence of such evil is what creates the strong current within their orb. It's as though Jessica had been protected. An observer of the dysfunctional lives rubbing all over one another, like too many fish in a tank. The crooked swimmers had seen the white girl and her Mother, and occasionally the old lady, but they'd proven years ago to serve no real purpose to them. The Mother's drug addiction had been respected, as it had proven to be a steady cash flow for her dealer, in essence, The Road Crew Mafia. Unknowing to the piranha, Jessica's subconscious had been continually passing judgment, putting the pieces together. Subliminally she knows so much about The Road Crew Mafia, ranging from the pawns to the players. That is why tonight, her subconscious will be used By the Shadowmen, as these entities will put some nasty people on notice.

Rodney Grimes is the first expendable to get stitched on this most eventful eve of dark takings. Jessica's consciousness is left at the door as the dark visitors, and their cat passes through the solid. The Brothers do not face the wall, taking their time. There's far too much shadow work in front of them; they follow Stitch's lead as the animal apparition moves like a starved, desperate lion. Rodney suddenly feels a tremendous weight upon his chest; the goons pressed hard into the mattress. The young thug feels the dark paralysis as he can't breathe or move at all. The dark, cold hands of The Brothers take hold. The current throughout his central nervous system is on the verge of overload! The teen struggles to breathe with the tremendous weight upon him; it feels like he's been filled with electrical sand. Rodney tries to open his eyes but can't. This human of no empathy feels the first Stitch of the supernatural needle; the slicing burn wreaks havoc within! The Shadow-Brothers execute their long-practiced trade with such precision and violence. This stitch work is not like the pattern they'd performed on Elsie; it's meant to terrorize. Rodney manages to open his eyes finally; the menacing tiger shadow is inches from his lifted face. As he registers the red glow of its eyes, he smells the foul odor of its innards. What feels like hours in the dark paralysis is only minutes in our reality, and the room soon lights up; as the dirty mouth of Carl Hester forms on the wall. The paranormal passage swallows the posters of naked women and famous hip-hop performers. Close to the end of the shadow sew, Rodney's spirit pops out! This darkened spirit doesn't stand peacefully by the edge of his bed. The Shadow of Leonard violently takes hold of the gangster's spirit. It turns it over in midair so it can see its stiff corpse, wide-mouthed, and the terrorized whites of his opened eyes! The newly formed shadow spirit watches the tiger pressing down on the flesh of his chest as the two red-eyed Dwarf silhouettes finish that paralyzing Stitch. Rodney's soon dragged down the tunnel. There's no light, happiness, nor the sounds of families having fun, laughing, loving; he's carried through an esophagus of violent chaos. This being only feels the evil that he's a part of. When he ungracefully comes through the other side, it's a night, and the Carneys are waiting, watching! These spirits are drunk and ready to help complete this night of terror! Bring the dark divine justice from the underworld for those who've bred so much terror in the light. Stitch and The Brothers drop this weak entity on the ground of the shadows; it sees the lights and feels the chaos, but there are no sounds. The Shadow-Brothers and their paranormal pet reenter the dirty throat to cross into the light. The head of Rodney's spirit is violently placed upon a stump. What is leftover of the tree the Brothers had been found swinging from while the tar had cracked. At the commanding nod of The Count, the shadow of George Wilson brings the sledgehammer down on the spirit's head; the sounds of laughter seem distant and underwater. The apparition's body is restrained within an old hog pen to lye still, to be licked and digested for all of eternity.

The Brothers and Stitch have reattached to Jessica's spirit. Their group shadow slithers down the hall. The flesh and bone of Rodney, a foot soldier pawn that has committed horrible acts against his fellow man, is now in an unexplainable coma. This teen had been used by top management of The Road Crew Mafia and has always been nothing more than expendable. Sixty-six other bottom-feeders get stitched on this eve and carried down the wretched throat of darkness. There's a muted celebration in the land of the shadows. For the dark reckoning is upon those of whom degrade the joy to be felt in the light.

Chapter 6

After a quick call to the nursing home, Martha wobbles to Jessica's bedroom. The smell of vomit is staggering. Jess is sleeping at the wrong end of her bed. There's a large puddle of dark emesis on the floor beside her. Jess wasn't drinking last night, Martha thinks to herself, and just as she's about to wake the teen up, she notices the flashing lights coming through the window. She's surprised by the chaos outside, as there are ambulances, fire trucks, and police cars smothered throughout the parking lot, their lights all flashing in a state of emergency. Disease Control vehicles, as well as media vans, are outside as well. Then she feels the eyes upon her. She turns around and looks into the marble soul of the dead cat. Although Martha has no idea what's going on, her instincts, on a primitive level, are telling her that Stitch is involved. The D.O.C quickly wakes up Jessica; "Are you alright, Jess? Did you throw up last night? There's something big happening outside; you should see the insanity down in the parking lot." The teen slowly gets up; "I'm at the wrong end of the bed again," she mutters to herself. "Watch out for the vomit on the ground, there Jess, but you have to see this, come here." "That's a daily occurrence here, Martha; someone was probably shot." "Jess, there have to be twenty or more ambulances down there." Jessica walks around the puke and goes to the window; "Your right Martha, something awful must have happened last night."

They go to the living room and turn the T.V. on. A live channel seven news report is just starting. A reporter stands amidst the chaos of emergency in the courtyard in front of the Broken Pavement building. The voice of an anchor introduces the reporter; "Taylor Stahl is live at Broken Pavement. Taylor, can you tell us exactly what's going on at Broken that has drawn such urgent attention from so much of the cities resources?" "Amanda, thus far, the Police are not letting anyone come and go from the apartment building; nor are they releasing any information about what has happened. I can tell you this though, several residents have said that this is not gang violence and that nobody is dead. Several young men, primarily teens, have supposedly been found in a strange coma. I've counted at least seventeen of these young men being wheeled out and taken to hospital by ambulance." "Is it possible that it's a mass overdose Taylor;" the anchor asks? "There's speculation; however, as I said, the Police and other emergency responders are not commenting at this time. According to one of my sources, a resident here, the Police are sweeping the building, floor by floor, looking for more victims. Disease control is here as well. I've tried to get a comment, but as I said, all the responders are tight-lipped; oh, here comes another one;" The reporter shouts! Taylor rushes towards the gurney. A young man is hooked up to an oxygen machine; his dark skin looks very faded. "Can you tell me exactly what's happened to this young man;" Taylor asks the two irritated-looking paramedics? Wanting to do her job a little too eagerly, Taylor jumps in front of them; her microphone goes flying as she's bumped to the ground. The medic doesn't apologize and just keeps on moving; he seems both focused and shaken. Taylor Stahl hasn't gotten to where she is by being a pushover. She quickly gets up and pursues the paramedics. As the cameraman is running, the image bounces, trying to keep up with the reporter. "Is there any indication of what is causing this; is it a mass overdose, a batch of bad drugs, perhaps?" The medics load the locked soul into the ambulance like robots. These are very well-trained medics and follow hospital protocol perfectly; not commenting to the media assures them that they'll not get into trouble. More than one medic has cost themselves their careers over the years by specu-lating to the press; these fellows are following the book. After the ambulance drives away, the siren screaming for all to move, Taylor straightens herself out. She does this very dramatically, as though she's gone through hell to do her best to get the people the story. "This is Taylor Stahl reporting live for Channel Seven news from Broken Pavement, first on-site, and first to report this latest tragedy from the infamous apartment complex. What has caused this outbreak? How many are affected? Why are the vic-tims all young men? What will be done about this; are the many questions I'll try and answer throughout the day! Back to you, Amanda."

Jessica turns the T.V. down and walks to the balcony door; "I don't think you're getting out of here at this moment, Mar-tha." Her boss joins her at the large window; a barricade has been erected around the property. Police are situated at strategic points to monitor who will come and go. Unknown to anyone, those who control the investigation agree that this strange phe-nomenon is most likely linked to drugs. The door-to-door sweep is being conducted in teams of five, four Police, and one health worker. By day's end, the media is informed that a total of sixty-seven young men suffer from the unknown affliction. Detect-ive Smith had led one of the investigative teams; his unit had discovered most victims, knocked on the most doors, and con-ducted the most interviews. After a very exhausting day, he has no idea of what has happened. Smith genuinely feels for once that family, friends, and roommates of the victims also have no idea of what's transpired.

Renee Sanders is not a formal employee of Disease Control but has a strong connection in the health unit. Renee is a doc-tor at The Better Sleep Clinic; she'd been given access to the scene. The Doctor has been permitted to observe. Renee spends her days helping people sleep better. At night she obsesses about the little-known phenomena she suspects is responsible for this strange outbreak of comas. Unlike the six other health workers accompanying the Police, asking the tenants an array of questions based on disease, Renee allows Detective Smith to conduct the interviews. The common thread she finds is that each of the victims had gone to sleep without any symptoms of infection. Inside, Renee secretly hopes drugs have played no part in this outbreak. Smith had been annoyed and short with Renee at first. Once she'd proven that she'd meant what she'd said, that she was there as an observer and would not infer with his investigation, the imposing detective had warmed up to her. Renee had told Smith that she feels he's on the right path and that she's sure some sort of common thread involving an illegal substance or toxin will show up in the blood work of each of the victims. Watching the aggressive form of questioning by the passionate detective only strengthens her initial feeling that these young men have been enveloped together in a strong sweep of the supernatural. Renee feels that Sleep Paralysis has laid upon these unfortunate souls. The Doctor had first learned of the little-known condition while at university. She had chosen it as her main focus; her teachers and peers had laughed at her, thinking she was a flake. The deeper Renee investigated the strange phenomenon, the more she'd linked it to the supernatural, and also that the power to be was content to keep this terrifying reality within a small community. Over the years, Renee has become obsessed with Sleep Paralysis and will use anyone or situation to further her studies; Martha Brown is one of these people.

Renee showed no signs of knowing Martha when the search and question team had entered the apartment. Smith had been very quick with the young teen. They'd met one another before; the aggressive detective hadn't bothered with her so-called friend. Renee had taken Martha aside; neither woman had revealed any information to the other. Renee was sure that something has changed with the Nurse and that she was holding back information. "They feel it's a mass overdose Martha, I've been told you should be able to leave within a few hours. Do you want to get together tonight?" Martha had had a tough choice to make; although she hasn't conveyed her true feeling for Renee, she's in love with her. The Nurse shares a curiosity about the occult with

Renee, but her true obsession has become the Doctor herself. It's been hard not seeing her, giving her the information she craves so badly. In reality, it hadn't been hard for Martha not to tell Renee that Stitch was in the bedroom. Her own life, career, and integrity were far more critical than a far-fetched relationship that would probably never come to fruition. The good Nurse had decided upon the emergency team leaving, that her relationship with Renee Sanders was over. Just as the young man had told her it would be in her office. Finally, around ten, Taylor Stahl reports that the sweep of Broken Pavement is finished and that the temporary quarantine has been lifted. Martha walks with Jessica. The place is still chaotic as people are exiting and re-entering. She knows she made the right choice in keeping Renee in the dark when in the mad scramble, the powerful young man from work passes her and gives her a reassuring smile. Unknown to her, he informally goes by The Third, or Three, to his Brethren and employees he is a Count; the grandson of the one who'd started The Never Sleep Swing Company. Jessica sees the smile and immediately blushes when her eyes meet those of the handsome young man that's dressed goth. Quickly he disappears, swallowed up by the underlying panic that surrounds them.

Deep below, underneath it all, the Road Crew Mafia meets. These humans are the true darkness that controls Broken Pavement. The war council is made up of Talon and Malcolm Briggs. The two brothers are the leaders, Talon being the C.E.O. and Malcolm the General. Their reputation with all those who live by the street's code is brutal; it's well known that there are no second chances with them. The sergeant of arms, the man in charge of weapons and gang warfare, plotting, and revenge, is Numbchuck. Numb is a massive man that puts fear and self-doubt into the hearts of strangers when he walks into a room. Chuck's reputation is formed upon brutality; rumors of him pulling arms off of people with his bare hands are much warranted. The Mind is just that, brilliant. This human could have done anything he'd wanted to with his life. His core was soured at a young age by the natural order of the street. The compassion shown to him by the

Briggs brothers had hijacked his jaded heart, thus forming the genius to their darkness. The Mind births schemes, hustles, and ways to operate around and above the law. Becoming a member or associate of this mafia came with having a camera situated in one's bedroom. Streaming live sex shows has produced a steady stream of income for the Road Crew. This had been the Brain's idea, and it's legal. This man's Mind is an essential element of this crew's success. D or The Dealer is in charge of drugs and maintaining the day-to-day operations of slinging throughout Broken. D is a terrifying man and has passed as many death sentences within these slums as anyone who's ever banged on Broken Pavement. The Dealer's bright green eyes are infamous, as they seem to glow against his very dark skin. A famous rap act wrote a song about D, the chorus line goes; "Don't pass his cane, Or you'll feel his rain; Cause he's the drug man, That brings the pain." This dark human uses an unnecessary cane made of marble that separates, exposing a very sharp hidden blade.

The final member of The Six is Doc., short for Doctor, or simply Dave. It was Mind's idea that his best friend Dave take various nursing courses at night. His scope of practice ranges from wound care to pill administration. Like any corner of this well-angled machine, throughout the years, the Doc has evolved. Davey is as skilled as many of the surgeons in the City at his a-septic self-made triage unit. This man has saved many soldiers' lives, but he has no diagnosis of what has dealt the Road Crew such a crippling blow in this dark moment. "Tal, I don't have a clue what's happened. I haven't had a chance to study one of them. My initial diagnosis would be a mass overdose or poisoning, but if this is the case, How? We're going to have to wait to hear it from the media." As angry as Talon is from Doc's lack of how; he remains calm. He's learned patience from the Lion over the years. "We've lost many of our best soldiers overnight!. Our legs that run the day-to-day have been cut off; Mind tell me what needs to happen now." The smartest man in the room takes his time; he pushes his glasses with tape on them up his nose. His entire goofy look intentionally presents an image of weakness to strangers. The others relax as they're used to this ritual; he's been this group's shelter during many storms. They know he has a plan. "I do not believe in luck running out my brothers. I believe in calculations of odds, risks, successes, and losses. We've accumulated much more than we need to move to the Island. Nothing but warm weather, fine cocktails, and beautiful ladies. I say we cash in and retire; live the good life, my brothers!" The others begin to cheer; all accept Talon, for this human knows the Lion will never agree to such an arrangement. The others are aware of this man and his actual power, but not the circle of other corrupt men that he rubs elbows with, the real power. They range from politicians to judges. They're all used to the trickle of illegal revenue they receive from the darkness of Broken Pavement. The Mind stares at Talon hard; he knows his long-time associate agrees with him and that it's time to get out before life bites back. "I know what prevents you, Talon, from agreeing with me. The Lion's strong, but I've created a slush fund for him over the past few years. More than two million dollars sits in accounts in The Far East." Talons eyes focus with controlled anger, the glance before the pounce; the others remain quiet. "What other cream have you taken from our cups, without consent, my Mind?" "Enough invested properly, that our disposable income, the net bottom line is over seven times what you all thought it to be. I've been preparing for this moment for many years. My contact within the passport company will need one week to administer our new identities. After which, we'll be free to cross any border, as different people." "Did you say seven times, my brother?" Talon slaps the closest to him on the back and lets out a very genuine cheer of laughter; the others follow. "Make the call, my brother. This crew is retiring!" This rowdy bunch mashes each other with hugs and affection. They agree to stay disciplined over the next week, to hole up together in what they call the penthouse. This space is an entire corner of apartments that have been connected, fortified, and with hidden escapes; it is beyond secure. A private conversation with Mind puts Talon on the right path; he'll shine The Lion over the next four or five days, getting him to agree. If the alpha of this Pride makes trouble, he'll be bled and made to disappear. The boss of R.C.M. had to be convinced not to do this later that night, as he'd felt this was the best way to handle the final hurdle. "Who knows what contingencies he's put in place, Talon, in case he suddenly disappears? We need to be able to leave and vanish under our new identities if were going to take him out." Talon sees the point and agrees. The call is made for new identities to be illegally crafted.

Resources are purchased to limit these men's need to leave the penthouse, food, drugs, and booze.

As intelligent as the Lion is, he's hunted hard on this day and come up with nothing. He searches the eyes of one he'd used to establish the Road Crew with when he was just a boy. The unspoken leader smells no treachery within the answers being provided. Talon plays the role, Mind instructed. The gangster's act is perfect, buying his crew the time they need to ready themselves for their change in life. "I'll think of a way to reestablish the well Talon, you boys play it smart and lay low. I'll find out who's behind this attack." Many rival gang membership numbers are much more significant than the Road Crew Mafia. This band of criminals has been kept low in membership and hanger-on's to limit the number of loose lips. Swift and brutal justice mixed with well-placed Intel about rival gangs that the R.C.M. has received from crooked members of the law have kept them in power on this street level for many years. In this dark moment, they're genuinely venerable, and not making those constant supply of payoffs would be bad for them. "I'll figure a way out of this, Talon, sit tight," and so the Lion leaves thinking he still has a paw on the pulse of the Pride. There's no way out of this for him, as the devil he has sold his soul to doesn't allow for early retirement.

Chapter 7

J essica watches channel seven programming, waiting for updates relating to Broken Pavement. There's been none for the past few hours, and she's feeling drained. During this chaotic day, she's found herself dazing off while trying to re- member what she'd have dreamt of. The realizations right there, like a memory, or a word, so close she can taste it; but it's as if a blank wall stops her from grasping this nagging impulse. There's a continuous sense of Deja Vu, the strongest of which she'd felt when cleaning the vomit up beside her bed. She'd stopped for a long moment as her mind tried to sneak past that wall. As fast it had come, it was gone, dead space, and as she'd sat there, she'd suddenly felt watched, not alone, and as the tiny hairs that cover her body had risen, she felt danger. Jessica had searched the room only for her gaze to find the marble eyes of Stitch. "They either get Stitched or Kneaded!" The phrase repeat- ing over and over in her head, in her grandmother's voice, and then; "Stitch will need you," in Molly Aiken's demonic voice. Just as the actualization came, the impulse was gone. It was right then that Jessica had suddenly remembered a face, a new one, the young man in the hall that had smiled at her. As she resumed cleaning the mess, strangely enough, she'd continued to think about him. Again there was a sense of Deja Vu, a strange cor- relation between the marble gaze and this new face. His clothes were marinated in Goth, not a cheap version like an outfit bought for Halloween, mass-produced, but the clothing of the genuine era. Jessica brushes her teeth, wondering if the reason she'd thought about the stranger is that his skin is light like hers and that he'd stuck out just as she would have to him. Neither could blend in with the loudly urbanely dressed, profanity spitting others who'd moved so aggressively around them. As Jessica lies in bed, drifting to sleep, she can't stop thinking about him.

Jessica's consciousness feels the brushing against her toes; soon, her chest is gently being kneaded. Nerves throughout her body gently burn as the paws push harder, but not aggressively, as the shadow's coaxing the conduit from the vessel. As it becomes harder and harder to breathe, her senses manage to force her eyes open. The red glow of its eyes initially masks its dark silhouette as it works. After a moment, her eyes become more atoned to the red darkness. Jessica sees the shape of the shadow cat kneading. She can't move as her central nervous system is paralyzed in this dark place between sleep and awake. Jessica struggles from within to move, to get oxygen, but she can't, and just as her neck shoots back, while her mouth stretches and her eyes roll back, she feels the massive internal pop! Now she's floating, looking down at her body, so rigid, neck up, eyes white, and the cat jumps from her chest, leading her subconscious to see the three shadows once again. They turn in sequence and come towards her. Again the teen wants to be afraid but feels familiarity as the Shadowmen go to her. Soon she senses the cold touch of the little ones and the decomposing smell of death. Together they float out of the apartment and to the stairs. Jessica's uncased spirit leads the three shadows to where they need to go. They pass some who live in the night, and as they walk in their rented light, these lost souls feel a cold presence. A momentary suggestion of the darkness that will someday find them. These addicts sense the shadows that will cleanse them of the many sins they've so carelessly committed. It's that quick hint of the rot, the smell, and the coldness that makes their skin crawl, as their controlled minds ignore the warnings of their subconscious.

The joint entity floats in front of the door; Jessica's apparition feels a sudden lightness as the shadow Brothers detach and make their way through the apartment. The three entities slither across the walls. Their dark silhouettes change shape per the angles and textures of the walls. The Penthouse is dimly lit, and their shadows may be seen for moments and then disappear. Five of the Mafioso are at a table, smoking weed and playing dominoes; each in their own way feels that cold dampness. Each smells the decaying rot instantly; however, each sub-conscious isn't aroused enough to register a fight/flight response. The dark entities move instinctively, sweeping each room. It's as though they're a pack of sharks in a dark ocean smelling blood that's slowly draining from a foot many miles away. Unlike the giant fish with rows and rows of razor teeth that bite so violently without any motive other than to feed, these supernatural shadows have a purpose when they attack.

The Doc's in a deep marijuana-induced sleep. Suddenly he feels the burning sensation starting in his toes, which quickly works up through his legs! The tiger-sized shadow of Stitch pounces on his chest! It feels as though a truckload of dirt has been poured on top of him! This paranormal insult is nothing short of a mugging of the soul! Doc's able to open his eyes, as every bit of grit he has inside pushes forth in this struggle to breathe! His heart hasn't had time to adjust to the body's sudden need for oxygen; the organ has just been forced into a state of panic! The glowing eyes are inches from his! The gangster can't move; he's been put into the dark paralysis in an instant. Doc knows he isn't dreaming. The gangster's able to scan the room with his wide-open eyes. He spots the dark visitors turning in the corner, and just as he sees the red glow of their eyes, he watches the three shadows disperse across the walls! Doc feels his wrists and legs firmly taken by their cold grips; from his peripheral, he can see the large dark heads of the little ones. With the most substantial, most frigid grip, the towering shadow is seen behind the heavy breathing paranormal pet that rests its weight on his chest. The smell that comes from the mouth of the shadow cat is unearthly. It's as though its breath is from a corpse that's been buried in pig manure. Doc suddenly feels his jaded soul thrust into the mattress. He tries to scream as The Brothers begin the supernatural Stitch, but there's nothing to alert the others of what's coming for them. Pinprick after pinprick, as they slice away, unseen through his flesh, as he struggles for oxygen, only able to claim enough to survive.

Soon the spirit of a man that could have done so much good is freed from its encasing—the Shadow-Brothers have control of this entity for eternity! Through the dirty mouth of Carl Hester, he's taken; the sounds of terror in the dark surround. This bad man sees the skulls and bones of apparitions appearing and disappearing in the misty fog of the paranormal passage. The deserving hostage to the darkness immediately feels the change in pressure once they come through the supernatural rift and into the Carnival of Shadows. It's been years since this newly formed apparition has been in a pool, but he quickly makes the connection. As the camp of shadows celebrates in anticipation of the new arrival, the sounds of the rides that move seem to be farther away than where they are as though immersed in a dark liquid. In the later years of Molly Aiken, new arrivals had come so rarely. The Brethren of supernatural have been putting the shadows that arrived the night before to work. Judging them in silence, to which ones are temporary visitors and which ones will be given to the tribesman.

The large shadow takes his arm and drags him towards the crowd. Soon he senses recognition, young men he has instructed, known, some he'd saved from injuries while being used by the Road Crew Mafia. In this darkened land, where the background is red at night, The Doc can barely make out the images of each distorted face. These young men look terrified as they stare at him in silence, the others cheering, their voices sounding so deeply immersed in the dark water of the spirit paralysis. The crowd of apparitions moves to a dark tent. Here are the new arrivals that had not done what they were told to during the day. These shadow rebels are bound to posts. Leonard points at one and appears to begin yelling. Still, the unfelt water texture prevents Doc from clearly hearing, so he lifts his arms to suggest he doesn't understand. Leonard nods to his Brothers. They untie one; this spirit had been so defiant, not a team player, so young to be so rebellious. Leonard violently takes the troublemaker in his cold grip. As the Carneys appear to laugh and cheer, the young shadow struggles. Its arm is snapped with ease, the shadow of a bone is exposed from within the apparition's appendage. Its scream is gurgled, submerged, just barely audible; Doc just stares, his entity in shock. The young soul is then picked up by its head, its shadowy feet kicking about, as it's shaken so viscously! Leonard stops and slowly turns, showing the suspended shadowy figure to his Brethren; Doc feels their excitement within the dark-mute. He spins the rebel's head entirely around in one quick motion, continuing to shake the apparitions head back and forth until the dark skull is torn clean off!Muffled cheers, he hears, as the head is handed to him. It senses a substance running from the unclean severance but sees nothing. The large one stands above, as Doc holds the shadow-head! It stares down at him, the eyes flickering between the red glow and real. The stare is of judgment, and then he feels a hand upon his shoulder. After turning, it meets the warm gaze of The Count; his surroundings go completely quiet. The Count points to him and directs Doc to follow; he does accompanied by the large one and another Shadow.

Doc hears the distant cheering resume once they're outside the barn, as three of the other new arrivals are about to be shown to the true darkness. The red and black background of this murky atmosphere is changing as they get into the carriage. To Doc, it feels as though the grey light suggests a powerful storm system is coming. This is how every day is in this existence; there's no rain, clouds, sun, or thunder, just a dank bleak grey. Soon after leaving the gates of the supernatural carnival Doc's senses return. The crimson background surrenders entirely to the grey. His captors are of the flesh; all dressed in clothing from many years past. He can now see their faces and hear their words. "You have come to us with a very sorry mouth." Doc looks into the now human eyes of the one he senses is their Leader, the one who may help him; "My mouth is...." Leonard gently touches his shoulder. Doc turns; he screams as he sees the swift movement, several of his teeth crack and break on impact, as the colossal fist smacks his open mouth! With no time to bite down, this one's jaw is broken! "You were saying about your mouth, don't worry, it's a short trip into savage land. There, your mouth will be taken care of, as well as that used-up soul of yours, Davey." Doc tries to maintain his dignity, wanting to make a deal, as he struggles to ask the Leader how he knows his name. He cannot speak, and while struggling to form words, he swallows a chunk of a tooth. The pain is severe as Doc chokes, causing blood to be spit as his mouth flares in pain. The Marshal, Leonard, and The Count don't laugh, as they do feel bad for what is to become of this lost soul, bad for the choices he'd made in the light to bring him to this dark path of absolute suffering.

The carriage turns off the dirt road and travels into the woods; the pathway is bumpy, and pain spikes with every callous traveled upon. This self-made doctor is no longer a confident man who'd preserved flesh for hire, for he's now a victim, kidnapped by the shadows, stricken by humility. Seeing the magnificent headdresses of the natives causes Doc to panic. Their necklaces of bone around their necks as they sit so proudly upon their horses. These mighty animals also wear paint to honor those who'd fallen fighting for their land. The sight of these warriors letting out a long-awaited war scream, as a promise of true sacrifice has been delivered, brings the new arrival to a place of shock. Doc feels the desire of paranormal primitive, as all these extravagantly surreal tribe Brothers' eyes feast upon his flesh, so ready to honor their gods with it.

The Count had met and got to know one of these warriors, in the light, during a land distribution meeting. Bear Wolfcreek had stood proud in his traditional headdress as the powerful white men had offered his people scraps from the table. Small sections of land that his people had lived on for many years before the settlers arrived. Unlike the other whites, The Count had felt empathy for Bear and was very impressed by how well the Native had spoken English and passionately negotiated for his Band. After the first night of negotiations, The Count had invited Wolfcreek for drinks. The two men had discussed many topics, ranging from religion to cooking methods. The most crucial issue being the lack of mercy and empathy that the whites would have for the Natives if they didn't succumb to their demands. "You're people will be hunted down, murdered, and broken like the other tribes have been Bear. I know that you're a smart man, and that's why you are the only Leader to have shown up to this rigged event. It's in you're best interests to become an asset to my people and most certainly not a liability." The Count had helped Bear achieve more land than what had been offered. Most importantly, a sacred piece controlled a large part of a river that was quintessential to preserving the Native's way of life. Bear's Tribe lived untouched on that land for many years until "The Other's," who'd banned together and rebelled against the white men's fancy weapons, had become much more than a nuisance. The dark magic and blood rituals of these angry savages had caused the new powers of the frontier to exterminate on a merciless level. The actual humans of this wild land were either butchered or broken. That was until the darkness began sweeping that generation of settlers, bringing their souls to the shadowland that exists behind the curtain of light. They'd either been Stitched or Kneaded. Once taken, they were either very fortunate to be kept by The Count and his Carney's. Those deserving were given to the apparitions of the dark riders. The worst of those taken from the light were provided to The Other's, the Demon-Riders. Savagely bad men like Carl Hester, who'd loved nor respected nothing, were given to the demons; that showed them true pain through eternal sacrifice.

The one whose face is painted differently dismounts his horse and comes to the carriage. Its teeth are so white and pointed; its dark eyes swell with an inviting creepiness. Everything from body language to facial expression suggests a strong desire to have the new arrival. The Count and Bear Wolfcreek embrace each other within a brotherhood that's been forged through time. They speak in a primitive tongue that matches the frightening appearance of The Warrior. The short conversation appears to be passionately friendly, as though a problem has been solved for both men. Once finished, The Count looks at Doc, who is grabbed by Leonard, having his face shoved towards the native apparition; "This one can't wait to show you stuff, Davey." Doc looks into its eyes circled by red paint on top of the black covering its face. The new arrival feels entranced by the hard stare, and as the apparition begins to speak, Doc smells the horrid stanching rot of a diet of wild flesh. "We'll take our time to fix the mouth, teeth, and set the jaw before...." It then touches Doc's forehead; "We fix the soul." Doc feels like a child; as Leonard takes him up, the large one whispers in his ear before he tosses him from the carriage, "I've seen what they can do, and they'll make it last forever. You chose to be here every time you went against what your Mother tried to teach you. She didn't come here."

After being tied and draped over a horse, the singing begins, the pitch is perfect, and through the chant, screams are sent out to honor their Gods! As the Dark-Riders take Doc deeper and deeper into these woods of the Shadowlands, a matching chant can be heard, getting louder and louder as they close in on the ancient village. Once within the smelling range of sacrifice, this chant becomes deafening! The gate is lathered in much variety of skulls, humans, and animals. Still, only the human bone that litters the entrance felt the actual pain of having their flesh manipulated to honor the supreme beings. These sacrifices had no empathy in the land of the light. Every night when this plane of existence turns from grey to red, their souls can be retrieved with incantations. The ritual sacrifice of a taken soul can be primitively tampered with over and over throughout eternity. Drums pound, as children point, they make faces at him; Davey's consumed by their primitive energy that suggests pure savage. The village smells of rot and smoke; the walls are marinated in bone and teeth. Doc must be dragged as his legs keep giving out.

The natives surround the large tent, where shrunken heads litter its outline; the Carneys had taught them this design of the home; as the natives had led them to use animal hide to wall them with. The shrunken heads are terrifying, with their little mouths wide open, revealing regular-sized teeth of many designs. The tent serves as a primitive dentist's office of ritual and torture; the occupants work their merciless fury without and form of anesthetic. A man covered in rows and rows of necklaces of teeth comes from within. Doc cries while feebly attempting to beg; dark urination runs down his legs. The Shadow-tribe becomes silent, for it's the sounds of the just sacrifice whimpering that will honor their true gods. The one covered in teeth steps to the side and points to the opening. Davey's lifted and carried through the entrance, as he can not stand. The deep thumping bass of a drum pounds from outside, magnifying the stink of rot and sweat; Doc puts eyes on the archaic-looking tools made of bone. As the Relics lie on the stand, seeming to vibrate to that drum beat, they whisper of the pain to be received. Soon he's strapped into the ancient dentist's chair, a gift from the Carney's; they aren't gentle with him as they begin the process of fixing his corrupted soul. Bone so viscously inserted into his mouth is only the beginning in this so-called afterlife, the hell that awaits his associates. The Dark-Riders will take their time with these long-awaited fixes; they'll cherish and savor each sacrifice like it is the first and the last. Each square inch of flesh will be so unnaturally tampered with.

Chapter 8

Burt Smith sits at his desk at home, starring at a picture of his Grandfather; he drops it, quite startled as the phone suddenly screams. The Detective was unable to sleep when he'd gotten home after sixteen hours of sweeping the ghetto. The computer forensics team has invaluable Intel for him. Once in the office, the Detective's very excited to hear that most of the victims from Broken Pavement had hidden cameras in their bedrooms. The forensic team had worked quickly to edit a video compilation. The silent film begins showing various victims making gang signs into the cameras; "Soldiers for the Road Crew mafia then;" the respected man comments; "Yes, sir." Soon the video clips into various associates having sex with random women; "We feel these young men live streamed these sex acts for money." Although we're unable to find a host site as of yet, we have discovered corresponding messages throughout their hard drives, communicating with one another that suggests this practice." Smith listens while focusing on the screen, "Sir, this last part of the evidence video is of the night before they were found." The young bangers appear to be struggling as they sleep. They breathe rapidly, then their bodies all go rigged, as their heads suddenly snap back. The screens cut in and out as though the feed is being disturbed by a change in energy. Their eyes can be seen; wide opened and terrified, rapidly moving back and forth, seeming to be scanning the darkroom. The victim's chests only periodically show that they can barely get oxygen, as though some unseen force is smothering them. The final stage of this strange convulsion shows their bodies being driven into their beds.

"Some sort of a seizure possibly then," the Detective asks his subordinates? "We just finished making this evidence video for you, Sir, and there's so much more to look at," the senior forensic officer answers. "None of you eggheads have any ideas outside of an overdose, then?" The youngest officer in the room clears his throat; "Forget about it, Jones," the senior specialist abruptly instructs. "It's okay, Officer Jones, go ahead," Smith advises. "During my final year in University, I did a paper on...." The others in the room shake their heads as the newest member of their team explains the strange phenomenon to their most respected Detective. Smith is in no mood to hear about supernatural fantasy. "Sleep what? What are you dribbling about, rookie?" "Sleep Paralysis, it's real, Sir, just not widely known about, look it up online." The prominent Detective aggressively steps towards the young officer, his extensive shadow washing over the much smaller man. The senior officer shakes his head. He likes Jones, but the pressure to perform, to problem solve, is eating at him. "You better find me something useful by the end of the day, or your going to feel every inch of me, do you understand? I don't have time for games or fantasy. I need fact!" Smith passes out on the couch in his office. Just after seven, he's awakened by a call. After washing his face and grabbing a cup of crappy coffee, he rushes to Light of Mercy Hospital, better known as LM General. Mercy is the only hospital that will take care of poor humans with no insurance coverage, like the sixty-seven young men from Broken Pavement. Other hospitals from around the city have donated equipment, supplies, and beds to Mercy to save face for the media, as the phenomenon is getting national attention.

Dr. Renee Sanders sips her coffee; she's just self-medicated. The pills will assure she'll be able to stay awake, focused, and just sharp enough to deal with her daily duties that begin in a few hours at the sleep clinic. The imposter spent the night volunteering at Mercy General. Renee fronted as a Good Samaritan passionately trying to save the young men's lives who've been afflicted by the strange outbreak from Broken Pavement. She doesn't care about the victims or their families. She'd only been there to feed her obsession, prove what she knows to be accurate, advance science by bringing Sleep Paralysis to the forefront. Renee's desperate to be the doctor who gets the acknowledgment from her peers by presenting non-debatable evidence of altered realities and that the occult and science are formed to one another. This unhealthy obsession manifested inside of Renee the moment her peers and teachers had laughed at her while she'd so passionately presented her thesis on Sleep Paralysis. The young student had thought the data she'd collected to be so hard, undeniable. Remembering the moment now causes Renee to feel sorry for her young self; how innocent and naïve she'd been. Every day since she's felt that moment's sting. Witnessing the unexplainable images last night that many respected doctors watched, documented, but could not explain, has brought her to the brink of proof.

At 4.07 in the morning, the first arm had just broken. The specimen hadn't screamed nor woken up; it was a domino effect, as eleven more cases in total had suffered broken limbs. Most of the medical staff of Mercy and the volunteers had witnessed the strange phenomena first hand. All had quickly heard as word traveled through the hospital. Renee had been one of the lucky ones who'd seen the head of the last specimen turn right around. As those dead eyes stared from above the back, some of her fellow doctors had vomited. The rest were so clearly shaken and unnerved, none having a legitimate explanation. Renee had had to leave the ward for a moment to regain her dignity. Not because she was going to vomit, but because she was so excited, and to see these arrogant doctors break like that had caused her pure joy. For an hour, the sleep therapist had sat with a handful of these condescending twerps, listening to them try and analyze what they'd seen. Words of nothing being spoken from trembling, stuttering lips. How badly she'd wanted to bring her theory forward, to jam it down their throats, but the timing was not right. Renee will be patient and meticulous this time. Eventually, she'll call a press conference, and by using the media, catapulting herself to stardom. This doctor of the supernatural needs concrete evidence linking these victims to Sleep Paralysis to catapult her life to where it should be. Renee had been trying to contact Martha all night. Although she'd only been using the nurse to collect more data, she'd wanted so badly to share the revealing moment with her. Many times Renee has boasted of her redemption to her so-called friend. "Their blocked thinking is the reason why science will only go so far. It's like cloning Martha; we can do it, but it's just not right. I mean, give me a break!" Unknown to this shallow human, Martha has taken a holiday and made arrangements for Jessica to take as much time as she needs. Martha's existence changed drastically the moment that strange young man had entered her office.

The core members of The Road Crew Mafia stand around the bed, each trying to comprehend the horrific sight that lies before their eyes. Doc's soulless eyes shriek in terror, seeming to stare in desperation into each of these gangster's souls. It's Doc's mouth that has brought about the sickly feeling deep within each of these very hard men. The fashion of which their associates now pointed teeth have somehow been manipulated through his swollen dead lips. The mouth so stretched as though there's an invisible vice suspending the point of entry. Some of the teeth have been removed and lay in the mass of blood that soaks the bed. There's much of the crimson splattered on the walls as well. They all wonder if the other or others had something to do with this. "Do we call the Lion or not Mind?" "Absolutely not, Tal. We review the video, dispose of Doc in a plastic barrel and hydrofluoric acid. We'll dump what remains tonight. We are very close to the Island, total freedom and luxury brothers." Malcolm Briggs, usually calm and quiet, suddenly cracks;
"Look at him, eyes wide open, dead, head up...no, I mean, his mouth what did this, come on what!" The Mind quickly responds, "Anxiety and too much cocaine, heart attack, I'd guess. You saw how hard he was hitting the candy yesterday, Malcolm.

Our good friend had a massive seizure, maybe!" "Someone had to have come into this room; look at his teeth!" Talon takes his brother by the arm; "How could they have Brother? I think the Mind is onto something. We have to keep it together." "I'll keep it together after we watch the video." A laptop is turned on, and now they're watching the Doc sleep. Just as The Mind says, it looks like their associate has a heart attack. His head shoots straight up, his eyes can be seen opening up so unnaturally, but then the video begins to fuzz, cutting in and out, as though there's an interference with the signal. Over and over, they watch the video, slowing it down; but can see nothing other than fuzz and quick in and out cuts of Doc struggling. The disturbance in the footage prevents them from seeing the entities that afoul Doc's flesh. The supernatural isn't discussed, as they decide how they'll move forward after disposing of the body. What's done is done; getting to the Island whole is all that matters. The Mind reminds them that one less partner means more for each. These jackals reassure each other that their long-time associate had ingested too much cocaine. Doc will be missed; the truth is that most of these bad men don't even remember his real name.

Jessica wakes up with her head hanging off the left side of her bed; a foul acidy smell quickly awakens her from her slumber. Jess isn't surprised to see the black vomit beside her bed. Before cleaning the mess, she goes to the washroom and then heads to the kitchen to put the coffee on; she then dials work. "Hey Jess, sorry to hear about your Grandmother." "Can I speak to Martha?" " She went on vacation Jess; she left you a message. Her exact words were that you're to take at least a week off or more and that you'll be paid. That you are not to be on the property." Jessica agrees and says goodbye. She now feels down, already missing the comfort her boss's company has given her. The teen has never felt so alone.

Just as she's about to stir an excessive amount of sugar into her coffee, Jessica finds herself starring at the tired reflection of her homely face in the metallic side of the toaster. Her messy long dark hair is bringing her down even more. The dark circles under her eyes make her look old and beaten by life. The phone cuts through the silence; the exhausted teen hopes Martha wants to invite her to escape. Jessica picks up and is told that her Grandmother's ashes are ready. While thoroughly cleaning up the vomit, Jess misses work that much more and can not help but think of Molly Aiken; her vomit had been very similar to this mess. Jess wonders if maybe she'd caught some type of virus from the late resident. After finishing, she takes a long hot shower, very intent on cleaning herself, just washing it all away. The hot water feels good. The soothing heat gently wakes up her cells that have been trapped in the growing prison of depression that has become her existence. Jessica thinks of that final birthday breakfast her Mother had made her; how tired she's looked. Jess felt so bad for her, guilty as she'd known her Mother had worked herself to a nub. The teen dries her skin, imagining what her Mother would say to her. "None of this is your fault, Jess; you are free. Live your life." The voice is as evident in her head as are the words valid. Upon wiping the steam from the mirror, a new face is revealed. Out loud, Jessica repeats the words, "None of this is my fault; I'm free. I will live my life!" Over and over, the lonely girl repeats these true-to-life words, getting louder as she thinks about what she now has; A job, money, and a familiar place to live. A strange and very seldom event occurs, Jessica smiles. Suddenly, the reflection she stares at in the mirror appears happy. The teen retrieves some of her Mother's never-used make-up. Jessica puts on a new face, deciding symbolically that she'll be beautiful and live beautifully; she never asked for this feeling of freedom she's experiencing.

Just as Jess is about to get into the elevator, ignoring the usual fear felt while migrating through the apartment slum, he's beside her. She looks to her right, and instead of looking to the ground, Jessica seizes this newfound confidence and smiles. The young man smiles back. "I guess we're neighbors, so hello," he sticks out his hand; Jessica takes it; "Hello back." Instead of letting go, youth stands there as though lost in a moment. Joe, the

Third Count's private security, lets go of a rare smile, which creeps Jessica out, and she abruptly lets go. Jessica's quite notable change of energy and facial expression is quite common for many who see Joe for the first time. As he's a massive man, his foundation is pure muscle, and his piercing blue eyes suggest a danger lurking beneath. "I'm sorry, this is my roommate Joe, and you can call me TC.." Jessica hesitates for a moment; the sudden opening of the elevator doors removes her from the shocked stare; "I'm Jessica, I...I'm sorry, I...." "Big Joe here has that effect on people, but I can assure you he's a big pussy cat. After you, Jessica," TC points her to go first onto the elevator; an air of high-class is evident in his chivalry. "Sure has been quite a lot of action around here over the past few days Jessica, is it always like this?" Jess feels giddy as she just stares at TC's outfit. The material is so beautiful. Pure class from a different era; black silk and velvet, the suits covered by a fantastic cape, and the letters NSSC are embroidered in large gold lettering on the back of it. "So, is it always this busy around here, Jess?" She loves the way he says her name, and just as she's about to answer, the elevator comes to a stop, and the doors open. Four teens join them in the small space; Jessica recognizes them more than a few times, inappropriate comments have come from their mouths. One takes notice of her make-up and the nice outfit she'd taken from her Mother's closet. "Looky look boys, Whiteys's got a body after all, and look at the way those tight jeans are forming to those luscious hips, some nice perky...." "Jess, do you know these gentlemen?" Fear and shame swell over her. TC reacts, "Either way, you gentlemen are getting off at the next floor." Without hesitation, The Count pushes the floor button. "Are you crazy White boy;" time stops as the voice of big Joe envelopes the small space. "I can assure you he is not boys." Jessica's heart skips a beat as the four youth of pure rude freeze, as fear overrides their usual cockiness. The elevator stops, there's a ring, singling the opening of the doors; "Here's your floor boys, now get out." The tone is controlled, but there's a hint of aggression in the command spoken by the giant. "This is our floor," one of them acknowledges as they all back out. "How quickly the fight leaves a dog that knows it will be broken," TC comments. "I don't know how they could fight with their pants that low in the first place," Joe kids. "Their pants don't have to be up high to pull a trigger," Jessica replies. "It's quite unfortunate that so many children are brought up without the compassion that teaches humans to cherish, love and respect one another." "You asked me how life works here, TC?" Jessica pauses, "It's murder, drugs, and thugs intimidating anyone who wants to live a normal life;" Jessica's tone is sad, genuine. "Believe me when I tell you this, Jess, life has a strange way of catching up to those who don't show respect. Many of our neighbors here at Broken Pavement are caught up in this vicious cycle, but what I'm wondering is how you've survived it?" Jessica ponders this carefully before answering and concludes she has no explanation; because it's unbelievable that she has. "I don't know how I've survived or endured this life, TC, but for sure, minding my own business, as in no drugs, boyfriends, and confrontation, has helped." The life of a mouse, the Third Count, thinks, as he's genuinely amazed and taken by Mollie Aiken's predecessor. "I have some laundry to do, Jess, and the rushed tour I was given of this magnificent place, well, I guess that wonderful man, Fred, forgot to show me where the facility is. I was wondering if you would like to accompany me at some point today and teach me the process of how one would launder their clothes at Broken Pavement." Excitement fills every particle that makes up Jessica Sworn. Then reality pulls the plug, knowing she's about to embark on a very long journey of taking many connecting bus routes to and from the funeral home. "I'd love to TC, but I have something I have to do. I'm afraid getting to and from the destination is going to take up most of my day." Not wanting to infringe on her privacy, he proceeds with caution; "What you have to do is none of my business, but would a ride speed up the process?" Jessica can count the times she's been in a car on less than all of her fingers. She hesitates as trust is not part of her DNA. The doors of the elevator open, revealing the lobby that is full of degenerates climbing over one another as they attempt to feed their desires. TC puts his hand on her shoulder gently; "I can assure you, Jess, my ride is much safer than this." It's his eyes that sell Jess, so genuine, inviting; "I don't doubt that TC, I'll take that ride, as long as it isn't too much of a burden." "As long as it's not a burden for you to help me with my laundry situation when we get back." Without speaking of the fear that has kept Jess from doing her laundry, usually, Cynthia would accompany her or do it for her, Jessica accepts.

Not one of the underachieving Jackals in the lobby comments as they exit the building. However, many have crowded out front, checking out the large black sedan that has just pulled up. Every detail of the classic car is pristine. It's as though its shell is impregnable to the expected effects time and use have on any automobile, protection based upon the labor of love. Those that have crowded around starring at the vehicle see a potential score. That's until they feel the intense energy of the giant that purveys them, quickly causing their immoral impulses to look elsewhere. The Third Count does not have to direct his driver, another of his beloved employees named Richard, to open the door for the girl. His polite mannerisms are of instinct. Jessica sinks into the car seat as though it was made just for her. As they pull away from the addicted needing eyes of Broken, she has no idea how much her life has just changed.

Chapter 9

U nlike family and friends of the victims of Broken Pavement, Detective Smith isn't about to compete in the waiting game that seeps through Mercy General's emergency room. The atmosphere is of intense desperation, as people push and yell, looking for answers. The highly motivated cop cuts through the line of frustrated civilians like a razor with rabies, ignoring their shouts and shoves; his badge quickly puts them into their places. "I'm Detective Smith; take me to a doctor that can give me an update!" The stressed nurse who's shed her caregiver status to serve as head of public relations gives him directions to a Doctor's office. After knocking and waiting too long, Smith stops a nurse that's walking by. Within minutes of rudely instructing her, he's sitting across from the intended Doctor. "No common links of drugs, nothing at all; you don't feel this was a seizure associated with a pharmaceutical that the victims all ingested?" Smith's voice is much louder than intended; never has this officer felt such pressure to solve. The older man clears his throat. He's shaken, not by the strong presence of this officer, but by the unimaginable atrocities he'd witnessed throughout the night. "We've done the necessary tests detective more than once that would link this strange outbreak to drugs. There's no evidence suggesting such a catalyst. Usually, our budget would not comprehend the level at which this unnatural epidemic has been observed and investigated. Every hospital in this city has donated resources and volunteers to help. Every test imaginable has been done, and yet a highly stringent and re-spectable panel of Doctors has no diagnosis." "How the hell is that? What makes this case so damn unique that every hospital in this city and their hotshot Doctors can't do their jobs?" Smith's becoming impatient as he feels the Doctor isn't telling him everything. The Detective pounds his large paw down on the desk, clearly unraveling the older man! "Last night, several of the victims, as they lay in a coma unexplainably around four in the morning began suffering broken limbs; one unfortunate soul expired due to a broken neck." "They were doing it to them-selves, is what you're saying, Doctor?" Smith watches the older man struggle as if he doesn't want to answer him, as though he's keeping a secret from him; "Well, get on with it!" "The limbs were just breaking on their own, Detective, I mean...." The older man, clearly baffled, pauses midway through the sentence. Again he's visualizing the horror of watching the young man's head just spin around, like a robust set of unseen hands had torn it right off. "There's no explanation how a man can turn his head right off, Detective! How could anyone explain such an unimaginable atrocity?" The Doctor then picks up a converter and starts the video again. He's watched it over and over, just trying to find something that makes sense. The chaotic savageness of these images is so real; they're surreal. Most certainly unexplainable; for the first time since being a child, this stone-cored man is frightened. Arms were lifting in the air on their own and just snapping! Bodies were moving in awkward positions as legs break and feet get twisted. It's the one who sits up, looking limp, and then his head spinning and being torn off that brings the fear. "You can't show this video to the media, Doctor." The fire in Smith's tone has been extinguished as he feels cornered. "DCB or The Disease Control Bureau is taking control of this case, Detect-ive, including all of the evidence. They will enforce a stringent gag order, and they're a mighty organization." In all his years of police work, the sweep at Broken had been Smith's first quaran-tine with the disease bureau; they'd more or less called the shots. "I need a copy of that disc, Doctor...." Suddenly the door opens, a beautiful woman with sandy brown hair and big green eyes enters the office. Her outfit wraps around her curvy body, and for a moment, Smith forgets the predicament he's in. "If that disc has anything to do with Broken Pavement Doctor, it will be coming with us. We're formally taking over the medical end of this case under the direct orders of the federal government; here's my warrant, Detective Smith." Burt reads the document and hands it back to the beauty that hasn't bothered to introduce herself. This woman exudes power as she stands with four solemn-looking men behind her. "Be on your way, Detective. We have our work cut out for us here, and good luck with your investigation. We'll keep you posted with what we deem is your concern, Detective." "A man died violently here. For all I know, it was a homicide, and I didn't get your name?" "I didn't give it to you, nor am I required to. Thus far, all medical staff involved have been prohibited from speaking of this matter to the media or anyone. You couldn't imagine how complicated we can make their lives or yours, Detective." Two of the suits aggressively step forward. "We'll be moving the victims to a private facility where you are not welcomed, Detective, now get out!"

After storming through the doors of headquarters, Smith heads straight to the Captain's office. Before he's about to argue his case desperately, his boss shuts him down! Smith is one of his biggest stars, is used to getting what he wants. The Captain tells him it's over and that Disease Control has taken over the case. "You don't get in these people's way, son, do you understand? You're on paid leave until this issue at Broken Pavement is finished!" Not one to be deterred so easily, Smith sits at his desk trying to figure things out. Desperate, he decides to start with Jones, the young computer forensic officer. "As far as I'm concerned, Detective, they suffered from Sleep Paralysis." "You have a copy of that disc." Although the young officer had been warned the evidence is to be sealed and handed over to disease control, he looks at Smith as a hero. He quickly caves, handing the department superstar a disc. "I could lose my job for this, Sir; we've been warned that it's hands-off. We're to sever all interest and move onto the next case, so please keep this between us." Smith assures the young desk-jockey it's their secret, thanks him, and goes back to his office.

He locks the door and closes the blinds; soon, he's immersed in the ancient phenomena of Sleep Paralysis. It becomes apparent to the Detective very quickly that the medical community is divided about Sleep Paralysis, as it's recognized as a severe condition by some and a frowned upon theory by many. Smith's surprised to learn that many different cultures for hundreds of years have dreaded The Dark Paralysis. Images of cats, witches, and other monsters resting on their victims' chests while they sleep are shared beliefs. There's a supernatural aspect to the disorder that leads Smith to believe this is why the medical community has frowned on Sleep Paralysis. Yet, according to different statistics, hundreds of thousands of cases are reported yearly. Three out of five people interviewed have suffered from Sleep Paralysis at least once. The reported cases range from one time to a chronic disorder. The latter is linked to more cases centering on the supernatural. Smith has never been one to believe in ghosts or hocus pocus. Still, he knows he must turn over every stone in this time of desperation to restore Broken Pavement to its natural habitat. A local doctor named Renee Sanders tops the list of professionals online that advocate for recognizing Sleep Paralysis as a severe medical condition. Upon seeing her image, Burt acknowledges her as the Doctor that had accompanied him on his sweep of Broken. Turning over his department-issued gun, car keys and signing the necessary paperwork lightens the load for Smith. Out of the spotlight now gives this predator more room to stalk.

Numb Chuck and D chop up their long-time associate's body so that it will fit in the plastic barrel. The smell is chemically putrid as the smoke rises from the barrel as the flesh slowly dissolves. There's no emotion in disposing of their associate in such a cold fashion. Doc lost, and at the end of the day, it means more money for them. According to The Mind, they're two, maybe three days away from reaching the Island and living out their years with nothing less than free will.

Chapter 10

J essica signs for the urn; her Mother had prepaid for many years before. She feels guilty as she looks at the absolute cheapness of the dull container that holds her Grandma's remains; it's identical to the one her Mother rests in. Tears stream down her face as she knows her Nana deserves a much more lavished ritual. Back outside, Jessica's numb flesh is tickled by a fresh cold rain. She watches as TC hands a police officer a card through the open back window of the black sedan. "I'm sorry young man, I wasn't aware, just doing my job as this is strictly a delivery zone." "No problem at all, officer." Richard opens the other back door for her. Soon the car is moving slowly through the busy streets. The rain seems to wash away the usual filth that marinates the constant shove that crawls over the rushed existence of city life. As some refer to the powerful young man, three can feel the sadness of loss that saturates the back seat of his car. "My father and Grandfather both rest in one of those, Jessica." The teen tries to remain strong, as she always with guard. Her Grandmother had always taught her from a young age to keep her guard up while living at Broken. The truth of this moment is too pure as it rushes to the surface; never has Jessica felt more vulnerable, alone, and unprotected! Jess's body shakes as she tries to keep the mask on, but there's no use, as the tears rush down her face in unison with the pleading sounds that come from deep within. "My Grandmother raised me. She deserves so much more than this cheap urn!" Three waits a moment, "That Urn is sacred, Jessica, for it's the final resting place of someone I can feel you loved very much. How it looks and what it is meant to others has nothing to do with the memories it contains to you. As a whole, it's symbolic of the cherishing love that you and she felt for one another. I would like to show you something if you would extend to me more of this valued and sacred trust you have so far." The strange use of dialect cuts the sadness; Jess unintentionally giggles. "Now you laugh, for what is so funny?" "I've never heard anyone speak the way you do. What I mean is people our age can't seem to get through a sentence without using profanity to strengthen their points, but it's not just that." "What else is it about my arrangement of words that's caused such an unexpected giggle than Jess?" "The way you speak, and dress TC, it's as though you come from a different time." "I don't hear you swearing Jessica, does that mean you have the ability to time travel?" "My Grandmother taught me from a young age that the use of foul words only exudes ignorance. She taught me that our beautiful language can be used in so many ways to get the point across." "I would have liked your Grandmother, Jessica. I feel that if you extend me a little more trust, that what I want to show you is something your Gran would have truly appreciated." Jessica's sudden feelings of excitement eclipse the overwhelming sadness. She ignores her instincts, deciding to commit. "It's extended, T."

The further south they get, the slower the traffic becomes. The uptown congested high rises of expensive living and corporate takeover give way to the brownstone housing—the price tags of these homes unimaginable to Jess. Never has she set foot in this part of town. Being a girl of poverty, her present surroundings make her feel small and uncultured. Jess looks down at her Mother's shoes, so cheap, just like the urn, and right then, she realizes how much more the world has to offer. Within miles of the City limit, flushing into the suburbs, the car turns right onto a private drive. Soon they come to a gate that fronts a huge treed corner lot. The letters NSSC are gothically presented in black cast iron across the face of the ancient-looking barrier, slowly it opens. The sadness has temporarily released its power-ful grip on Jess as anticipation massages its powerful claws with each rotation of the tires. The graveled drive is long and sided by manicured gardens and trees that provide complete privacy. Finally, the sedan comes through the tunnel of seclusion and anticipation, giving way to a courtyard of fountains and statues. Jess recognizes the carnival theme, NSSC; The Never Sleep Swing Company. She looks at TC, and through his window, the image of the most spectacular mansion unbelievably looms; large stones and carved statues of carnival-themed memories marinate the space. "What is this place, T, and who are you exactly?"

Repetition allows Renee to fit the older patient for an oxygen mask without any thought relating to the task. Her mind's en-veloped in the realization that Disease Control has taken over the Broken coma cases. Even worse is that her old classmate Dr. Dianne Bonnie is heading up the task force, or more so, will be covering up the truth. She and Dianne had debated vi-ciously about the validation of Sleep Paralysis in med school. Renee understands the necessity to protect the public from the fact, dispel and discourage certain conditions, and avoid mass hysteria. If the masses ever knew the truth about unexplainable crib death, it would create chaos amongst young mothers. How could any parent feel safe at night, knowing that the shadows could take their innocent baby's ability to breathe away? Her ob-sessed journey of understanding and validating Sleep Paralysis has been as much a moral struggle to Renee as getting her col-leagues to listen to her. Her initial goal had been to raise funding to treat and explore this supernatural realm. If one could see through her flesh and peek into her mind, they'd see an obsessed human way beyond wanting to help. Over time Renee's obses-sion has reduced her to wanting to be the Doctor who proves that the occult and science can exist as one. This drive to prove her colleagues wrong, to validate what she's known for years, keeps her research moving forward without regard for the safety of victims of the Shadow-Paralysis. Renee's passion hasn't been overlooked late at night. When she thinks she's alone at work using the clinic's equipment to study these unfortunate souls, she's constantly being watched.

Renee welcomes the buzz from her intercom; "Dr. Sanders, there's a Detective Smith here to see you." "Give me a minute, please; I'll be right out." Without really knowing if the dimensions of the mask will allow the senior to get better sleep, Renee okays the fit and prematurely sends the patient on its way. She rushes into the waiting room; Renee and Burt quickly reintroduce each other and head back into her office. "I'll get right to the point, Dr. Sanders, the other day you volunteered your time at Broken. The only reason you did so was to further your studies of Sleep Paralysis?" Having watched the prominent Detectives imposing demeanor during the sweep keeps Renee honest; "That's true, Sir." "No doubt in my mind, you were at Mercy the other night and witnessed the unexplained phenomenon of the broken bones, specifically the beheading?" "I did." "Although I've only read so much online about Sleep Paralysis and yourself, I have a strong feeling that many of your colleagues believe this unproven condition is a joke. Thus they treat you as a joke, Doctor."

Only a few nights ago, this comment would have sliced through her core. After watching more than one Doctor throw up during the bone-breaking atrocities at Mercy, her skin had toughened, knowing she was on the verge of factual evidence. Rather than getting defensive, Renee only smiles at the aggressiveness of the big cop's words. "You're here for a reason, Detective, and said you had a point, so get to it." "Watch this." Within a few minutes of viewing the footage the computer forensics team had edited; Renee Sanders feels tears of triumph come to the surface; Sick lady, Smith thinks to himself. Renee wipes her face and takes a moment to reflect once the video is finished. Finally, she has undeniable proof that Sleep Paralysis is real. What humans deem as nightmares is kitten's spit compared to the absolute terror that supernaturally lurks within the shadows. "May I make a copy of that disc detective?" "That depends on how we can help each other, Doctor." "I'll give you any information I can, Detective." Renee feels a dangerous shift in energy as Smith leans towards her from across the desk. "I'm sure you know, Disease Control has taken over this case. It didn't take me long online to conclude that that bitch over there is partly in the business of discrediting you and your hocus pocus. I grew up at Broken Pavement Doctor, and I intend to save as many of those young men's lives as possible! I could have easily been one of those hoods who are drawing breath from a machine." Although his voice is calm, it's slathered in mean, suggesting a primitive instinct that will stop at nothing. For the first time, Renee decides she'll take on a partner. She pushes her intercom button. "I'm feeling sick Darlene, cancel my appointments for the rest of the day."

The Third Count opens the large wooden door for Jessica; "Welcome to Shadow-Estate, Jessica. Over many years my Grandfather constructed this place in honor of our family business...." "The Never Sleep Swing Company," Jessica finishes. "That's right, Jess, you've heard of us then?" Nodding her head, Jessica replies, "Who hasn't, so you own it then, T?" Jessica feels his warm touch gently take her hand. "Follow me, please, Jess." The ceiling is very high in the long corridor, and the walls are covered in art. Some are modern, most are old, but all of the canvases are lathered in a carnival theme. Jess tries to slow down. She wants to look at the art, ask questions, but Three keeps gently pulling her forward. Soon the teen hears laughter and music; the large hallway opens up into a gymnasium-sized space. Jessica stops; she pulls back and begins laughing. An overwhelming feeling of happiness immerses her, as the Carney's are practicing their various crafts throughout the ample space. Jess thinks about Nana and her obsession with the invisible Carnival show that had entertained her, watching it on the white fuzz, laughing and giggling like a little girl. Jess hadn't been raised to believe in ghosts or Gods. Still, right now, as she watches Carney's work, feeling the synergy of these talented humans, in a sense, she experiences a spiritual awakening. Jessica Sworn knows that her Grandmother had been watching something, a foreshadowing image of where she stands now.

"I don't own this, Jess," TC steps into the practice space; "We all own The Never Sleep Swing Company," The Third Count shouts! Cheers and screams echo throughout; this young man is loved by his employees. These genuine people are working on skills with the intent of bringing temporary joy to strangers. Most of these humans had watched the eighteen-year-old they know as their leader take his first steps as a baby, had watched his Grandfather, The Count, bounce the young boy on his knee. That great man had built so much more than just a fortune company; he'd made a family. Many years before, they'd all accepted the young girl, Molly Aiken, as one of their own, even knowing the darkness that surrounded her. This is why the Carneys all step away from their practices and make their way towards Jessica Sworn. They are all humbled, as they all know The Brothers are near, watching from the shadows, being led by Stitch. Three takes her hand once again and leads her towards them; they greet her one by one, all-knowing her name. Jessica's overwhelmed by the friendliness and the respect she's receiving from these strangers that all feel so familiar. The only other experience this young woman could compare to this moment was meeting her Mother's co-workers at her wake. For the first time, Jess feels a sense of community. This foreign feeling is so inviting to a girl that's spent so many years hiding in the shadows. These people are not glamorous or beautiful; they're real, genuine; for sure, they're her kind of people. More and more come from the sizeable sprawling backyard, all waiting, so full of anticipation to meet her; only one hasn't taken that first step towards it. That person is the other human that's so linked to the supernatural darkness of the occult. Lady Dark had taken on the title of her Mother two years prior. Her Mama's brittle-aged spirit and body had finally succumbed to a long battle with the shrout. The special women had been born with the gift of sight. Many would refer to it as the burden of the dark. As her Brethren welcomes the one associated with what lies beneath The Never Sleep, Dark watches the giant shadow of the black cat slither about. Its energy is so intense and so dark. It's unseen and unfelt by the rest as its silhouette passes through and about, brushing itself against the unknowing; never does its red glowing eyes leave the stare of the psychic. The Third gives her a nod, signaling that she goes and waits in the occulted heart of the Shadow-Estate. Three leans into Jessica's ear and whispers, "Come with me, so what is going on here can be explained to you." Jessica nods in agreement and follows him.

Soon they're headed down another large hall; every corner and inch of this space is covered in the art of ancient gothic. Just before they are about to go down a set of stairs, Jess stops; "How do all these people know me, T? What's going on here?" "You'll have to trust me, Jess; just please come with me." Jessica feels an immediate change in energy once they're in the basement. The walls are made up of large stone, and the décor is of Mid-Evil relics that shout out of the occult. The temperature is suddenly cold, and Jess smells an underlying foul odor of decay. "T, am I safe?" Three stops and gently put's his hands on her shoulders; he then turns her towards a large painting. "Do you recognize this person, Jess, and what she stands beside?" "That's Molly Aiken, and Stitch, you knew her?" "I loved her, Jess, as did most the people you just met; the ones that knew her." "Just met T, but seem to know me; how's that?" Three takes a moment; he can feel her nervous energy. "Jess, how have you been sleeping since meeting Molly, or more specifically since bringing Stitch home?" Jessica's ready to run. What kind of devil play is this handsome young man involved in, her mind flashes? "Why were you at Broken T? I mean, you couldn't have been there by accident. What do you want with me, all of you? How do you know of Molly or Stitch; I mean, of how I've been sleeping?" Jessica, about to run, freezes as she hears the slow creak of a door opening. The dimly lit creepy space is now marinated in a warm red glow, coming from the room that has just been revealed. A dark silhouette comes from within; the shadow's gait is slow and gentle as though approaching a wild animal that's ready to attack.

"You're here, Jessica Sworn because you have to be. This world is full of evil, and you know that. Many humans that you grew up around at Broken Pavement bring this evil forth. These lost souls do not care about the unnatural unbalance they create in our existence every day with unjust murder. Getting what they desire by any means is in their DNA, for they have no respect for human life." The older woman comes into plain view, she's tiny, and most of her body is covered in a dark cloak. Her large light blue eyes glow in the reddened darkness. "Come into my space so that you may understand you're new existence, Miss Sworn." "What if I don't want to?" "Whether or not you want it doesn't matter, Miss. Sworn. Through your contact with Molly Aiken, those in the shadows have attached themselves to you. I'm afraid that your life has been given to them now." So many emotions are flooding over her, she looks to Three, and he nods as though prescribing trust towards the old woman; "You're all part of a cult, aren't you? Is it my blood you want?" The Third Count takes her hand in the darkness. "You're one of us, Jessica, now go with Lady Dark and find out what you need to know. I'll be waiting right here for you. I promise you have never been safer." It isn't his words as much as the conviction in his eye that shoves Jess towards it. "There's so much I'm going to show you, Jess," and so the door closes on a life that can no longer exist, opening another that will reveal what watches and waits in the darkness.

Chapter 11

"You don't even know what floor the room was on, where you saw the girl with your friend Doctor?" Renee honestly can't remember; "I can't explain it. It's as though it's right there Detective, on the tip of my mind, but it's blocked." The sketch artist is finished. "How's this, Miss. Sanders?" Renee takes the drawing that she feels is the conduit. She and Smith had been to Martha's apartment and office; the secretary at the True Care nursing home had refused to give any details to Martha's whereabouts. The nervous woman had finally threatened to call the police. "I am the police lady!" Smith had replied very aggressively! "Then you can wait for them to show up, and they can explain my employer's right to protect the privacy of their employees, especially without a warrant." Renee was surprised that the bull of a man had keeled so quickly. Smith had explained his temporary vacation from duty right after they'd left the property. "This looks like her for sure. I only saw her for a moment, but I sense this is her." The gears of Smith's mind grind to associate as he recognizes the girl but can't place from where. He knows this spike of De Ja Vu will remain with him, harassing him, but the connection is lost, blocked. "Thanks, Remy, for meeting us here and doing the sketch; please keep this to yourself." "Burt, none of us in the department understand why you've been asked to sit on the sidelines, let alone the case being shelved." "Doesn't matter, just keep this to yourself." "Of course, Burt," the small man leaves after they shake hands.

The desperate Detective shakes his head as he stares at the unknown girl in the picture; "A conduit," he says out loud just before taking another sip of his beer. "You saw the way those bones broke, Detective. Why are you still denying the supernatural?" As he begins to speak, he points his finger at the Doctor; "Stuffed cats that enable spirits to crossover and extract the souls of the living by entrapping human bodies with Sleep Paralysis... is a lot for a sane person to wrap their minds around, Doctor." Renee is growing quite tired of wasting time explaining what she knows, what has consumed her life. She only needs one thing from the Detective to bring it all together; "I've fulfilled my end, Detective; I feel it's time I get a copy of that disc." "When we find the stuffed cat and the girl Doctor." "I'll scream, remember you're not officially a cop right now. I told you I have a charity event I must attend tonight. If I remember anything or get in contact with Martha, I'll call you, I promise." An impulse strikes the cop, part of Smith's deserved and earned success has always been channeled through following his intuitions. "I'm not letting you out of my sight, Doctor; if you agree to take me to this event, we'll stop at my place so I can change, and I'll make you a copy." Renee agrees as this is the exact arrangement she'd been leading Smith towards. The Doctor had no plans of going to the Shadow-Ball at all, especially dressed the way she is. Using people has become more natural to her than helping them.

Jessica immediately feels the dark energy throughout the room of occult and a strong familiarity within. Jess senses a presence, as though they're not alone in the room. "Relax, Jessica; what you can't see has no intention of hurting you." "I can feel we're not alone; I mean, I'm not crazy. There's something in here with us, isn't there?" "You felt their energy every time you visited with Molly at the nursing home, didn't you, Jessica?" As though the older woman's words are an unknown code to an impenetrable safe, her mind begins to piece it together. "I did, yes I did, but that's not the only time Lady Dark." Jessica takes a deep breath; "That's it, my child, center yourself, feel what you already know. They didn't hurt you then, and they have no intention to now; this is just an introduction." Jessica feels the gentle touch of the clairvoyant as the older woman takes her hands. The shaking slows as calm seems to flow through the soft, weathered flesh, allowing her mind to work unaided. Slowly, images and words spoken flow as one, the Carnival and the cat, Stitch, and Molly. "They either get Stitched or Kneaded," Jessica gasps as she touches the scratches on her chest. "The gentle scratches of a loving cat that's been playing a little too hard, Jessica." The witch's voice is barely audible, but to Jessica Sworn, never have words been spoken so powerfully. Right then, through the red glow that hangs like fog throughout the room of ancient, she sees the dark silhouette of the cat. The image is quick as it rubs its shadow on the wall behind her host to the occult. "You can't ignore it, Jessica; they've chosen you. From the moment Molly Aiken put her eyes on you, felt your energy, the shadows took you in." The Witch moves to the side and points to a large rectangular shape covered with a black velvet blanket. "What I'm about to show you is the true history of what has chosen you, or more so the cause; I need you to be strong." The teen feels the wings of butterflies flapping within her core while the velvet mask is removed. The black eels slither through what is left of Carl Hester in this world. The bad man's Skelton is wrapped and shackled with a black chain in the large tank. The water glows a light pink as the Shadow-Brothers appear behind the encasing of the occult. The entity of Stitch jumps from the wall and into the giant Shadow's embrace. "The large one in the middle is Leonard. While in the light, he'd found Stich near death and nursed the cat back to health. The two small ones are Joey and Felix. They're twins; these are The Brothers, our Brethren in the shadows." As the three sets of eyes open, the red glow of their pupils takes Jessica's mind to her bedroom, she remembers. Molly Aiken's predecessor is no longer afraid, for she knows these are the Brother's her Nana spoke of. Jessica remembers standing over her rigid body while the shadow of Stitch weighs upon her chest. Jess hears the pop as her spirit breaks free, followed by the cold touch of the smaller one's shadowy hands. The smell of decay enters her nasal as they form with the shadow orb. "Your pureness and innocence give The Brothers the direction they need to put things right, to bring balance." "Balance to what Lady Dark?" "A balance to our plane of existence, Jessica. The Brothers abduct the souls of those that are evil and transport them into the darkness. Those that are taken have unnaturally robbed so many good humans from the light, thus unbalancing what should be." The dark Eels that had just appeared many years poetically glide within the pink tone of the tank. The blackened apparations gain their energy and size by rubbing their supernatural flesh upon the bone of a bad man. Lady Dark gives Jessica a shortened version of what reporter Max Stahl had documented so many years before in Green Bud. The book's rights had been solely purchased by The Count, as this exclusive story was for only some to read, but never the masses." With the glow of their eye upon her, Jessica Sworn asks, "But why wouldn't he want to tell this gruesome tale and make people aware of the Dark Paralysis?" The Witch takes a moment, as she knows this will shift the young girl's existence even more; "The Brother's are not the only Shadowmen Jessica." Jess feels the chill of dread; "They're not?" "The Skeleton of Carl Hester shackled is symbolic of the general public's mind as a whole, not thinking or obsessing about Sleep Paralysis in these times Jessica. You see, the Dark Paralysis has always existed, and since the beginning, has created hysteria amongst humans. The Shadowmen in older days were honored and worshipped as Gods of terror. By fading this truth out over time, humans have been able to live without this prominent fear of sleeping. These other Shadows I speak of are the invaders, the bad ones, the darkness that needs no direction, the ones that steal baby's souls in the night. The ones we call Demons! The only purpose of this Legion is to turn the wheels of evil, which creates such hate in the hearts of humans. As this bone is contained in this tank, there's no common knowledge of the demon's existence; thus keeping their darkness to a minimal Jessica."

Three's nervous as he waits, wondering if innocence is accepting her fate or not? What will he do if Jessica turns her back to them? The idea of taking her hostage and bonding her to a life of an unwilling conduit is unbearable. It's this thought that's kept him from a proper sleep since Molly Aiken had accepted her presence. "My Count, I must talk to you," the leader of this Company welcomes the interruption; "Yes, Joe?" "I'm sad to say that Dr. Sanders has made a horrible choice; I wish I'd been wrong about her." Three takes the phone from his bodyguard, knowing what he must do. As the leader and sole heir of his family's accumulated wealth and power, and most importantly, the Company's responsibility of controlling The Dark Paralysis. The Third Count must destroy the life of one to save many. With this type of power comes great responsibility, and as a young leader, this is one of his toughest tests yet. His father, The Second Count, had given Renee Sanders her scholarship personally. He'd handpicked the promising young girl from high school upon interviewing several candidates. Over the years, unknowingly, Dr. Sanders had made so many discoveries that helped the Company harness its control over the paranormal darkness of Sleep Paralysis. Unfortunately, over the past few months, Dr. Sanders had given into the temptation of feeding her existence. The Doctor had been attempting to withhold data. Now it's time to contact the other young lady her father had presented a scholarship to that year. One whose mind is just as brilliant as Dr. Sander's; but much more disciplined. Before Dr. Sander's existence is changed, her life of being a scientist of the sleep removed, the Third Count must be sure. "How bad is it Joe, can it be fixed?" The large man slowly shakes his head, and through the red glow, the sadness is revealed by such expressive eyes; "Tell me, Joe." The head of security for The Never Sleep Swing Company hates these moments; just like his father, three doesn't handle this type of disappointment well. The depression of such a crushing decision will significantly affect youth. "Dr. Sanders will have indisputable proof of the Dark Paralysis. This Detective Smith will give her a disc that validates what she's known for years but hasn't been able to prove. Renee's already promised Taylor Stahl an exclusive interview. She'll launch the Dark Truth, unknowingly injecting mass hysteria into the hearts of all humans. The Legion of Darkness will have unlimited paranormal access to a mass of willing and unwilling conduits. Thus once again, My Count, just as Lady Dark has warned, we'll all be in The Dark ages." Such powerful words from a man he trusts more than any other puts forth the confidence in his heart. TC dials the number of Dr. Dianne Bonnie, the other young woman the Company has invested so much in. The Company's power and influence had positioned her high within Disease Control to protect the masses from the truth. "Dr.Bonnie here." "This is The Second's son." Dianne needs a moment, for this is the first time she's been contacted by him directly. Once alone in the darkness of a custodial closet, she feels she'll be able to provide the attention this powerful man needs. "Yes, my Count," her voice is shaky, as this very confident woman feels humbled. "Let me begin by personally telling you we're all so proud of the job you do;" tears glisten in the darkness of the closet. "Unfortunately, your former classmate, Renee, hasn't been doing so well as of lately." "How so, my Count?" "Dr. Sander's has managed to gather the proof she's always hunted. Rather than bringing it forward to her employer's or handler's, she has decided to chase personal glory by securing an exclusive interview with Taylor Stahl." "I understand, my Count," how badly Dianne feels for Renee. Although discrediting her colleague has always been part of her duties, she's always cared about and respected her. "Renee will be at the Shadow-Ball tonight; unfortunately, I need you to attend our benefit in a much more professional manner. Joe will be by soon with the evidence you'll need to expel her from her duties as a Doctor." "I understand, my Count." "I'm passing you to Joe to make arrangements. Once again, I'm so proud of the choices you continue to make; they never go unnoticed, Dianne." "Thank you, my Count." As TC passes the phone, the young, powerful man begins to battle the conflict that eats away at his insides, as he knows Renee Sander's life is about to be erased.

A few hours later, Jessica sees him in a chair outside of the room of occult. She feels humbled by the knowledge she's gained of his lineage, but at this moment, he seems troubled, stressed. "I'm ready to serve The Never Sleep Swing Company, my Count." The Third feels an immediate release, for this arrangement of words is precisely what he needed to hear. As attracted to him as Jessica is, the fantasy that's begun within is finished. The conduit now sees him in a much different light; "What will you have me do, My Count?" "Tonight, you'll be my personal guest to the Shadow Ball, which means you'll have to have a dress made." Soon Jessica is immersed in pampering she could never have thought possible....

The nails are filed,
As the hair is done.
A new face applied,
An old life is gone.

Chapter 12

T he Shadow-Ball is a must-attend by the rich of The City. Much of the talk within high society is about meeting the new CEO of the Swing, the Third Count. The Second Count had kept his son's identity private and protected from those that would want to control or manipulate him. Three has no intention of giving these humans any of his time. TC's Father and Grandfather had greased enough palms for a lifetime. The Ball is held at The City Convention Center. The facility's grand room can easily accommodate two thousand checkbooks; the back right corner is reserved for Carney's. Three hundred very different and unique personalities will take over that space of the grand room. The Carney's will ever only be themselves, outsiders. Each will go as they are, whether game master or Fire Breather. Beneath the tax write-off and hob-knobbing of the rich, this night is to celebrate what The Swing company has provided for years; escape pleasure and protection for the masses. Three will mix in at a random table, very careful not to draw attention to himself. His Father and Grandfather had taught him that doing so only puts a target on one's back for the jealous hearts of haters. This type of greed will saturate the Shadow-Ball.

Jessica spins around again as she looks at herself in the black and royal blue gothic gown one more time; she really can't believe it's her reflection. As happy and pampered as Jessica had felt during her transformation, her mind had kept swinging back to the skull and bone of Carl Hester. The teen's skin crawls as she thinks of the Eels gliding in and out of the bone. According to Lady Dark, the slimy creatures had just appeared one day, spawned by the supernatural. Her mind's eye continues to show her the Shadowmen who'd just appeared in the ancient room. The realization of already meeting them, having felt their presence in Molly Aiken's room. Before Lady Dark told her what her role would be in the Never Sleep Swing Company, she knew what it would be. Jessica feels the struggle to breathe before the pop and the cold touch of the Dwarf's hands, suggesting gentleness and danger. The teen's only sadness comes from the realization that she and Three will not be together. Lady Dark hadn't said this. Upon the knowledge gained of his family's true power, she'd come to her conclusion that she could never be a proper match for him. Yet as she is led down the large spiral staircase, watching the crazy characters that make up the Swingers, she feels his eyes upon her. Within seconds she's able to trace his powerful gaze to a corner of the large parlor room. As he sits on his throne, she sees the expression of surprise, as he noticeably takes in the beauty that has been brought to light through the makeover. Jess can barely believe it herself. How natural the high-heeled boots feel that has changed her normal unnoticeable gait into the glide of an exotic cat. In one motion, he stands and snaps his cape into place. His appearance exudes confidence bred by tradition. The Third Count is entranced by Jessica Sworn, even more so than when he'd first been made aware of her existence. Now that she'd accepted her dark role within the company, he's drawn to her. Lady Dark had forbidden him to look underneath the covers to let Jessica naturally fulfill her true destiny. Through her ancient teachings, this young man had fallen in love with Jessica Sworn many years before. As attracted to her as he is, the mentoring he'd received would not allow him to fully have her until marriage, as it had been in the days of old. As badly as they both want to take each other's hands, they don't. "You look different, Miss. Sworn;" "Thank you, my Count; you look the same." "You and I will ride to The Ball together, Jessica, but first, we must go to the back of the property and surprise a very old friend."

Billy sits at a table doing his best to find the same puzzle piece he'd been looking for, for the past two hours. The old Carney is frightened he'd dropped it on the floor. His old body has been imprisoned in the wheelchair for years; thus, retrieving the missing piece as proven in the past would be nearly impossible. The Game-master could call for help, but dignity has always stood between him and the call bell. The sudden knock at the door irritates him as usual, and it's early today; "I'm not hungry, I'm busy, leave me alone!" "I know you wouldn't have talked to my Granddaddy or Pa that way, William Jones;" Billy's attention snaps into place; he's shocked to hear this voice! "My Count, I'm so sorry, I didn't expect you...." "Still stuck in that chair, I see." The Carney's all-time cash leader in games is in tears, as to him, he's in the presence of nothing short of a demi-god. "How can I humbly serve you, my master?" "Tonight is your night, Billy. You'll be dressed in your game master's suit, as you'll be personally accompanying me to the Shadow-Ball." Bill Jones is a live-in; he does not like to be seen by anyone in his wheelchair; "I'll do anything you ask my Count." "You'd better fellow!" Once cleaned and dressed by a nurse, The Third Count pushes Billy out of his private quarters in the back of Shadow Estate. Billy's dressed in his one-of-a-kind suit. This humble man feels a profound sense of pride as horns honk from the long line of cars that contain his Carney Brethren, who all consider him nothing short of a legend. "Who are you, my beautiful young lady?" "My name is Jessica Sworn." The older man looks back and forth at the Third Count and the bright new face that sits across from him in the back of the Limo van; he has a mischievous little grin. "Jessica's, Molly's chosen replacement Billy." "Oh..Oh..Oh..I...I, I did, dd...." It isn't just frustration that quiets Billy, but the sudden visual of The Brother's hanging from that tree. The Game-master can hear the cracking sound of the black tar and see the shadow cat that had followed him that night. After a moment of gaining composure and settling his tongue, Bill asks the question he's been meaning to for some time; "When can I sit down with Lady

Dark, my Count?" "And what is it that you need to know so badly, William?" "I'm tired of waiting, my Count?" "Waiting for what?" "For them too," the older man nods his head towards Jessica, "To...tttt...take me over." TC puts his hand on Billy's leg, "We'll talk about this when the nights over, okay, my old friend." Billy, not wanting to embarrass himself, further nods in agreement.

The long line of cars enters the side passage to the private underground parking lot of the City's Convention Centre; they're the only party that does so. The exclusive have-lots that have been invited to the ball must park or be dropped off in the public parking sector of The Center. There's a strict no drop-off zone out front that's strictly enforced on this night. The original Count had demanded this unusual action from the Center years before. This simple inconvenience forces the snobs to have to walk down the sidewalk from the parking lot. They stand out, as would pink flamingos suddenly showing up for the first time to a public park and having a group mating session. For these noses in the air, humans, the walk is below them, humiliating. Although it's become the opening ritual of this highly anticipated annual event, none are ever happy about it. The media shoots them as though they're on safari, pursuing wild boar. As the rich are shown their overpriced reserved seating, the Carneys commence in their opening ritual. A tailgate party in the parking garage inside the back of the Convention Center, no other group of this size is ever permitted to do so.

Rowan Montieth walks toward the young Count with It. This young man has just achieved a status none other have in that World; Lady Dark is suddenly consumed with a feeling of dread. Her 7th sense picks up a very sudden foreign energy from the large one in sunglasses who walks beside the well-to-do young man. Rowan extends his hand; "The Third Count, I would like to welcome you to my humble abode." Three takes his hand, "Thank you, Mr. Montieth, for allowing us to use the garage to get our night started." He then releases the human's hand and extends his towards It. The Visitor looks down towards the human; Its goat-shaped eyes underneath the dark glass would have directed the human to pull its hand away quickly. Rowan cuts in quickly; "My associate, Mr. Fade, does not like the touch of human or other people's hands. Anyways I would like to wish you a great night, and I...." It buds past the main servant to those that dwell in the Darkness; "Keep up the good work, Boy." It then gives Rowan a look and walks away. The most powerful human in That World looks back towards The Third Count; "I'll be signing a nice cheque for your charity tonight, Sir, please enjoy your ball." Like any human who has a chance encounter with one, Three is jaded by the Visitor's energy. A feeling of dread and confusion brought on by an internal primitive instinct has sent a strong message of danger to his cells. As he watches his brethren enjoying themselves so much, he forgets and quickly rejoins them in their moment of celebration.

Detective Smith sits at a table quite close to the large stage; he and Dr. Sanders share the spot with five of her co-workers. He's enjoying their conversation and, for the time being, has forgotten the crushing pressure he has been under over the past few days. The loud noise that accompanies a large crowd of people that have all been drinking takes Smith's attention away from the conversation at the table. The Never Sleep Swing Company has just entered the large banquet hall. All are taking their reserved seats in the far back corner. Their loud outfits that stand out in the sea of fancy tuxedos and expensive gowns disappear one by one into the dark shadows of their placement. "Who are they, Renee?" "Those are the members of The Never Sleep Swing Company Detective; the Carnival is the host of this very exclusive charity ball." Renee pays no attention to Smith's response as she watches the loudly dressed Carney's disappear into the shadows. She thinks of The Second Count and how he told her how proud he was of her when he'd personally awarded her with the scholarship. Renee knows she should be sitting down with her boss the next day instead of Taylor Stahl; she owes it to the clinic and the ones that invested in her at such an early age. How could she ever explain all of the illegal research she'd been doing after hours on those whose lives have been terrorized by Sleep

Paralysis? There is no explanation for her lack of ethics to further her research. Renee again decides she's in the safest place she can be, and she has a man of the law to protect her. "Detective, I have more evidence to show you after the ball if you're interested?" "Absolutely, Doctor." Just as he watches a clown whose juggling bowling pins disappear into the far dark corner, the music stops, and a masked Dwarf in a tux takes the stage. The short human walks funny, and its body is too thick to be a child's. It's the hideous mask covering the face that takes his attention; it looks to be made of bone, and its theme is saturated in tribal voodoo. The voice that welcomes those in attendance is thickly deep and misplaced to the stunted man behind the mask. He speaks of one of the company's primary missions, explaining the importance of long-term care. The short host talks about the lack of beds needed to provide proper quality care for those in the final stages of their lives. "Our Company have built and own many of these homes. The Counts dedicate millions every year so that humans can live out their lives with dignity and comfort. Much of what you donate tonight will be returned in tax savings, and please remember one day; you may need one of our beds!" The crowd stands and claps loudly as the little fellow announces the commencement of the evening activities. One act comes from the darkness after another; their colorful outfits seem to spit out from the shadows. Soon swords are being swallowed as fire is being breathed; magnificent illusions are performed on the occult stage. A magician stares at Smith as he walks to the stage. The tall man in the top hat looks evil with his devious smile. His act is breathtaking as he dissects a volunteer from the crowd, eventually making her head disappear. The magician never seems to take his eyes off of the Detective during his feat. After this, the hall goes dark, and the curtains close on the stage. A vast ray of red light cuts through the darkness, producing a crimson spotlight in the corner where the Carneys sit; suddenly, there's a black cat in the middle of it. The red light moves with the giant cat, the shadow illusion seeming to rub its darkness on the silhouettes of the rich ones that sit in its path. The shadow entrances the crowd, and just as it reaches the stage, the curtains open!

A little girl sits on a bed; the covers are black, she wears a white nightgown. The gentle sound of a flute cuts the eerie quiet. The crowd gasps as the cobra slithers from under the bed. Its body is black, the markings that form the diamond pattern are red and gold, for none of the spectators outside of the Shadow-Company know if the reptile is real or not. The snake's now in a coil in front of the girl. A rasping breath of fear rushes through the rented room. To those unknowing, it appears that the surreal serpent is no illusion. Its head moves in a rhythm that seems stitched to the increasing tempo of the flute. The little girl's eyes look towards Renee as she lies down on the black bed. Her innocence seeming to invite the cobra unto her flesh. The serpent glides sensually across the bed; the crowd reacts in hush shrieks as though they're watching something far too taboo. Her eyes never leave Renee's, and as the snake coils up on her chest, the little girl closes her eyes. The flute stops, and right then, the snake goes flaccid, and the curtains close. There's no applause, only shock. Dr. Sanders feels the darkness around her; she just knows the primitive exhibition was directed at her! She's ready to leave. The curtains reopen, and the little girl bows to the crowd; she holds the limp snake. Her being safe revitalizes the event; as hands clap feverishly in relief. Next is the art show. "I need to go to the washroom after that," Smith announces to the table. Still shocked by what he'd just watched, he doesn't register the look of fear on Dr. Sander's face.

Those in the dark corner had seen the act many times. They congratulate Fiona as she sits back down beside her mother, Lady Dark. None of these humans question the supernatural but rather accept the occult into their hearts once they become attached to the Swing Company. Jessica can't take her eyes off of Fionna like the others she'd anticipated fang to flesh. Jess feels the warmth of his gentle touch graze her arm; The Third Count stands beside her. "I need you to come with me, Jessica." she stands and follows; they move through the bunched-up tables unnoticed. "Dr, Sanders are you enjoying the evening?" Renee looks up and knows for sure right then that the cobra act had indeed been for her, for there's no mistaking the quite recognizable face of the son. "Not so much, my Count." "This is the girl you've been looking for Doctor, may I present Miss. Jessica Sworn." Renee looks for the Detective. Her cells are in a state of perpetual hope that he may come and save her. "Nice to meet you, Doctor." Jessica extends her hand, Renee takes it; "You as well." Three lowers his head towards their hands. "You showed so much promise when you were young. How disappointed my Father would have been in you and your irregularities over the past while. If you'd shared with us, we might have shared with you." "I won't talk to her, my Count. I'll share everything I know with you, I promise!" The Count shakes his head; "You think there are things you know that we do not, my dear? You haven't felt our constant watch, have you?" Jessica pulls her hand away as she watches the tears run down this lady's cheeks. The others at the table have taken notice but say nothing. They're all curious as to what their co-worker has gotten herself into. Renee's strange behavior at the clinic has not gone unnoticed. "Your investigations and your career are finished now, Renee; there's no making things right when you've done it wrong for so long." The art auction is interrupted for a moment as Dianne instructs two of her officers to place her former classmate into cuffs. Right then, Detective Smith gets back to the table. "What are you doing? She's done nothing wrong!" "This is none of you're concern, Detective; to my understanding, you're on a leave of absence right now, so do yourself a favor and continue it!" Smith keels, knowing he's in no position of authority in this awkward situation.

As Renee gets walked out of the hall under the curious eyes of the rich, Dianne explains why Renee's losing her medical license and the criminal charges she's facing. Just as they get to the underground parking, there's a moment between them; "What were you thinking, Renee?" "Let me show you the footage, my case Di, from one Doctor to another." "We've already gathered the proof from your apartment Renee, all of it. I've seen so much more than you have; I know so much more than you do!" "What's that suppose to mean, Dianne?" "I know about the Dark Paralysis. It's always been my function to keep it in the corner, in the darkness. I wish you would have done as you were told, my old friend." Renee's put in the back of the police car, knowing she deserves what's coming to her.

Those in attendance quickly forget about the minor drama as the lights dim down to near darkness. No longer feeling welcome at the table anymore, Smith leaves. A very tall man takes the stage. Unknowing to the have-lots, he's dressed in a Never Sleep Gamemaster's outfit. The Carney's cheer very loud, and the rest in the room follow suit! Ben, as he's known to his Brethren, uses his hands to quiet the noise. "It took me many years of hard work to reach the level of Gamemaster within the ranks of The Never Sleep Swing Company. There's no learning institution that one can obtain more knowledge about life. At times it's a vicious path, and no other human has ever learned more than Billy Jones, our companies greatest gamer of all time!" Those in the Darkness erupt around him; all cheer his name as the old man feels appreciated for the first time in a long time. A vast screen drops behind Ben on the stage. "This is why we're so proud to announce our latest attraction here at the Shadow-Ball; this ride is a game-changer!" The screen comes to life. Computer engineers are shown designing and formatting the soul of the new ride, as carpenters and welders build the shell. Soon a group is shown walking through the entrance of the ride; they come to a chair. Although the humans in the room cannot fully experience the 3-D brilliance of those on the screen, the magnitude of the virtual reality displayed is surreal. Now Ben screams, "Shadows will dance, as people scream, So buy a ticket and dare to dream!" By the end of this video of humanly engineered impossible, all of these guests know The Swing is in line to profit greatly.

Jess watches as the Third Count puts a mask of bone on. TC then commences in pushing Billy Jones through the sea of ramping human excitement and onto the stage. Ben loudly clears his throat and signals for the crowd to quiet. "With great honor, I introduce you all to the man that inspired us to such greatness, even to think we could program such an experience; this is Billy Jones." The Third Count bends down to Bill's ear, who's overwhelmed, and not close to accepting his new role as a respected hero. This humble man is a true legend within the vast network of The Never Sleep Swing Company. "You're coming out of retirement, my old friend, as the master controller of your ride." Somehow the cheering and applause get that much louder as The Count pushes one of his favorite humans besides the microphone. "My family has always been in the business of improving the lives of humans." The crowd becomes silent as all realize that the new CEO of the Swing is behind the mask. "Bill Jones was with my Grandfather the day The Brother's were found; he's been with my family for years. His honesty and loyalty are of that stuff that has helped The Never Sleep Swing Company become so much more, and that is why we've named this virtual experience after him. Billy's Chair will be open to the public within a few weeks, as our season to entertain commences!" The Third Count bends down and hugs this man he loves so much. "Wait until you feel the control station that could only have been designed for you, my old friend." "You honor me so, my Count, thank you." Three looks to the crowd again; "In the name of Mr. Jones, all monies made from Billy's Chair will be used to build and maintain Nursing homes! As The Never Sleep Swing Company, our most important mission is to improve the final experience humans must face, and that is the lonely and frightening journey into the Darkness!" A magnificent-looking building suddenly appears on the screen. "This is the generic design of our new line of Nursing homes; the brand will be called "Our Gentle Touch," or OGT. The building has already commenced of twenty-seven of these fantastically economical hospices, where all care is free and available to those who need it the most!"

Chapter 13

The Third Count ignores the cheers from the crowd wanting him to remove the mask while pushing Billy back to his Brethren's corner. The lights go out, and the stage comes to life as though it's a bright red artery, and the masked Dwarf announces the presence of pure rock royalty. "And without further to do, will you all welcome Rev Lighting!" The metal legend walks out with his hair down low, just as the heavy metal riffs of the guitar hush the older crowd. Rev's here to honor the member of The Never Sleep Swing company, not the rich. Within the shadows of the corner, The Third Count removes the mask of primitive and takes Jessica's hand. His gentle touch requests that she stands, and as she does, he completely wraps his entire being around her! The Count retreats quickly, though, for as soon as he'd become lost in the moment he is found, and there's an awkward exchange between their eyes. Jessica is perplexed, as she's never had a relationship with a boy, but she feels he's attracted her. Jess decides to leave it alone. They sit in quiet sorrow as Rev Lighting performs at his best and purest as he'd been commanded to do. "No drink or drugs before this show boy," is what It had told him. While the sober, most unique rock voice begins to rip, the checks start to be signed and collected. After the fiery performance of a legend and the gourmet meal is consumed, a highly respected big band begins to chime out the elevator music. This tempo brings forth old money to the dance floor. While they happily move, they don't notice the

Carney's leaving the hall. Over four million dollars has been collected. The Third Count gives Bill one more hug. He tells him
how thankful his family is for his years of dedicated service and
that he can't wait to see him back to work.

Once in the back of the black sedan, The Count looks at Jessica;
to her, he seems very stressed, as he had during the evening.
She'd caught him stealing glances at her over and over. "Jessica,
Joe, and I will accompany you to your apartment for what I hope
is your last sleep there. According to Lady Dark, you've accepted
the Carnivals proposal." Jess agrees; however, she's afraid she'll
not be able to sleep at all. The sedan moves quickly through the
barren city streets. Jessica never noticed the shadows that lurk
everywhere, as the vast lights from the condensed buildings
breed them as soon as her view changes. "If you drink this, Jess,
it will help you sleep." "I don't drink alcohol, TC." "I don't drink
either, Jess, nor do I ever presume that anyone else does without
asking first. I did presume, however, that after Lady Dark spoke
to you, that sleeping may be difficult. That is if you truly believe
the story of The Brothers." "I know what she told me is true,
TC. I saw them in her room. I can feel them now; I've felt their
presence since I first entered Molly's room. What I can't get my
head around is why they've chosen me?" "They sense the same
purity and innocence in you that I do. Being that you have been
raised in Broken Pavement, a world that breeds such evil and
anger, it makes you special." Jessica thinks on this for a moment,
"Fine, I know my heart is true, but how can you and the rest
even think I can be strong enough to show them the way." Three
smiles, again he feels an impulse to hug her. The attraction he
feels towards Jessica is magnetic. "Only the strongest of people
could grow up amidst such hate and stereotyping to what your
neighbors assumed you are and remain as focused and caring
about your family as you did. This is why my family, The Never
Sleep Swing Company, would be honored to have you as one of
our own. So be brave, you are brave; because my Brothers are
your Brothers, Shadow or whole." Again the conviction in his
eyes draws Jessica entirely in. Although everyone had been so

friendly to her at work, she'd still felt like an outsider. For the first time in her life, Jessica finally feels like she's genuinely a part of something. The teen's facial expression changes from unsure to confident; she takes the drink from The Third Count and swallows it back.

By the time the car pulls in front of the lobby of Broken Pavement, Jess feels sleep drawing her in. She's having trouble keeping her eyes open. Just as they get out, another car pulls in behind them. Four large men dressed in black t-shirts and jeans get out; each has guns that are pretty noticeable in their shoulder holsters. TC looks at her; "Those men are with us. Being that this is your last night here, Jess, we'll take every precaution to ensure your safety." "As you please, my Count," Jessica very softly replies, as she's ready to sleep. Three instructs two of his bodyguards to help Jess walk as her legs appear to be wobbly. The nightcrawlers in the lobby quickly spread at the sight of the organized and armed party. They pass through and waits for the elevator without being accosted. Although they do not respect much, the presence of these men suggests nothing in the sort of an easy target. By the time they're at Jessica's floor, she has to be careful with her mouth, so close to unconsciousness. The conduit's unaware if she's speaking in her mind or out loud of the intimate feelings she has for The Count. "I'm so glad I met you. I know you would never want me, but I'd do anything you wanted me to." The running of her make-up magnifies Jessica's uncontrollable loss of dignity. Although The Third Count feels a powerful attraction to Jessica, he can't convey this to her. He feels very badly for her in this venerable moment; he hopes she'll not remember this the next day. Jessica's role in The Never Sleep is vital. It requires such discipline that there'll probably never be a safe place for them to become lovers. Jessica's asleep before they get to the apartment door; once inside, TC instructs them to place her in bed, as she is. The four bodyguards patrol the hallway; he and Joe will wait in the kitchen until Jessica awakes.

The sensation of her nerves tingling as though an electrical current is pricking the ends of them raises Jessica's awareness.

This time when she feels the gentle touch of the Shadowcat's dark paws slowly making their way up her legs, subconsciously, she knows what's happening. Soon Stitch's supernatural claws are felt kneading her chest, and as the weight increases, making it hard to breathe, she feels her head jerk up! Jessica opens her eyes; she's looking into the red glowing pupils of The Shadow Cat. Just as the weight becomes too much to breathe, feeling she will explode, Jessica looks to that right corner and sees The Brother's backs. They're facing the wall, and then comes that pop! Jessica looks down as she feels Stitch rubbing its being on her legs. She sees her body so rigid on the bed, her mouth and eyes are stretched wide open, and her head is raised up and as forward as far it can. The Brothers turn in sequence; their glowing red eyes are upon her soul. Her subconscious is armed with the knowledge received from Lady Dark though this time, Jessica bends down and picks Stitch up. Jess commands her soul towards them. As they're about to form, she passes the Shadow Cat to the large one and welcomes the cold touch of the supernatural Dwarfs.

News from Mind that their fake identities were ready had spawned the sudden discipline of the remaining five members that are the nucleus of The Road Crew Mafia. Each refrains from any substance and goes to bed early. All day, they'd been anticipating a visit from The Lion. Surprisingly it seems they'd be able to leave without dealing with his potentially deadly wrath. As Malcolm had suggested, instead of partying now and risking a surprise visit from their vicious master, discipline could ensure a neverending party. So in this late hour, each has managed to shed the anticipation of freedom for an unsuspecting sleep.

It's The Dealer that feels the burn first. The Shadowcat's claws dig into his legs before it pounces on his chest. The human struggles to breathe as the weight of supernatural justice is tremendous. The Dealer's eyes are wide open as his head suddenly jerks up; he's inches away from the red glow of the entity's angry eyes. This one will not be kneaded. The thug can't move his body, only his eyes, as he's immersed in the Dark Paralysis. Soon his glance finds the right corner of the room, and there they are, with their backs to him. They do not wait for his soul to escape; there's no mercy for this one. He can smell the rot of its breath. Just as it digs its claws in deep, The Dealer feeling as though he's under wet cement manages to move a finger. He feels a sense of waking up and then comes the first cold touch to make sure he can't. The human glances towards the Dwarf-Shadow; its icy grip is firm! His eyes dart to the left as he feels the grip of the other Dwarf, and then he feels the large dark hands of the big one coldly wrap around his ankles. The Dealer is paralyzed yet feels the stitching that commences on his left side first. With each prick of the supernatural needle, he wants to scream as the pain burns so badly. Although the sew job only takes minutes in our reality, The Dealer would have spoken of a ritual that had taken hours. Near the end, as his body is, so Ridgley pushed down into the mattress, he sees the light come from the right wall. Just as the Dwarf pushes the thick thread through an ear, completing the paranormal ritual, The Dealer can no longer breathe. The banger fights internally to survive, and just as he's about to succumb to the relief of death, he feels the pop and is looking down at his body. The foul spirit stares at the disgusting mouth that's formed on the wall; he feels their cold grip again. The entity struggles in the darkness as it fights against The Brothers, but there's no use, as it's now deep in the esophagus to the Shadow-land. It feels the screams and agony of many tortured souls that have been dragged into this ghostly plain. The Dealer's spirit feels the change of atmosphere as they come through the tunnel. This dimension is thickly moist, and his vision is marinated in red. He feels thrown to the ground. The Shadow gets up, it's about to run, and just stops; he takes in the silhouettes of the Carnival. Its sense of hearing is muted, as though it's under-water. Other Shadows come to him; one passes him the outline of a cup. The Shadows appear to be drinking, he takes a sip, and there's a sensation of swallowing beer. The Dealer follows these dark apparitions to a large tent. Once inside, they take a seat amongst many other Shadows and watch the show. The new arrival can feel their cheering; it can sense it as the sexy silhouettes dance on this supernatural stage. The terror inside of The Dealer eases as it enjoys this segment of the nightmare. Soon it feels the sensation of being patted on the back and spoken to. Finally, it recognizes their presence, as some of the soldiers found in the coma. It wonders if Doc will come to him.

The Shadow-Brothers, led by Stitch, work their way through the ghetto-penthouse, seizing the souls of each of the remaining core of The Road Crew Mafia. Stitch brings forth the occult justice in the weight of all the innocent souls these men have taken by placing it upon their chests. During their turn, each of these bad men awakes suddenly as their heads jerk up, their mouths and eyes stretched open, as the Shadowcat's eyes burn red. The weight on their chests, getting heavier as their hearts sped up, each struggling to breathe. They'd each seen the entities of The Brother's approaching them as the foulness from Stitches guts smothered their sensation of smell. Each felt the coldness of the Dwarfs touch first before the large one took their ankles. All try so hard, but none could scream as the supernatural stitching ritual commenced. The Dwarfs take turns using the paranormal needle, as they both enjoy stitching the deservings flesh to the mattress. Both Shadows have perfected their technique over the past few days, working quickly and neatly while administering the maximum burn. Although their targets can't make noise, their eyes silently scream in agony and confusion.

Numb-Chuck's spirit had proven to be the most challenging taking these Shadow-tailors had ever taken on. His spirit had fought the cold grip of The Shadow- Brothers, right to the final stitch. His defiance had caused a very sloppy stitch, causing the flesh more pain, but this powerful human had taken it no problem. Its spirit was as big as Leonard's. Unlike the other members of The Road Crew Mafia, it's not going down the dirty throat of Hester without a struggle. The apparition twists and turns kicks and bites, but it doesn't matter how much it fights. Stitch digs its claws into the Shadow's head as the Brothers drag it through the paranormal passage. Numb-Chuck stands in the red thick. Leonard touches the new arrival gently, and in that muted under-water sound tells it to follow them to the big tent. The dark spirit of Numb-Chuck senses its Brother's as they watch the dancing; he's relieved, as are they, for he is the fighter.

The Shadow of Leonard offers the newest arrival a drink. It takes it and feels the sensation of swallowing beer. It feels comfortable that it's in a dream, as the sleek female apparitions have made their way from the stage. The dancing Shadows provide the sensation of touch as they rub their darkness on the new arrivals. Their blackened silhouettes appear naked in the red atmosphere. Leonard's beside Numb, being so friendly to the large one. The Shadow-thug has no idea that soon, the sun in this dimension of shadow will bring about their new reality. The Mind keeps trying to speak to what he senses are the Shadows of the only family he's known, for his subconscious senses what's happening. It feels that this dancing of Shadows is a lure. It senses that they're all waiting for something, and as it speaks to Malcolm and Talon, who can hear its distant words as they float in the thick moistness, it knows they're doomed. The light of this existence begins to implode its grayness throughout the moist thick red. The Shadows in this paranormal state take on their form in the flesh, turning from the darkness. The Mind's not surprised to see the wickedness in their eyes. The Carneys are like a pack of coyotes, starved and circling, not letting on to whether they'll be siring or devouring. "The Road Crew Mafia, you call yourselves," none of these thugs replies. "Welcome to our Carnival of spirits; come outside with us."

Leonard looks eye to eye with Numb-Chuck. "It's alright, big man; what's done is done." The muscled-out gangster is used to intimidating people with his sheer size; he senses a change in the deer-licks attitude, he's senses aggression. They follow the man in the cape outside; hundreds stand in the middle of the booths and amusements. The atmosphere is very grey, as though there's a significant storm coming. Talon's had enough; "I don't know what is happening, or if I'm dreaming, but I want to know where the hell we are? Who the hell are you queerly dressed people? The Count walks to the center of his Brethren; "Their fearless leader wants to know where they are, and who we are, my Brothers and Sisters!" The leader turns and laughs mockingly towards Talon; "And we're the ones that are dressed so queerly, are we? Look at yourselves with your pants almost hanging down to your knees. With all that money you have so greedily hoarded from weaker people, one would think that you could have purchased a suit? Instead, you dress like one of our side attractions!" Loud laughter drives Talon to take out his gun and walk to the Count; without hesitation, he tries to pull the trigger, it won't budge, as if the safety's on. "You and your cronies are in no position at the present moment to be asking questions. I'll tell you this boy; this is not a dream, and you couldn't be any further from home!" A loud cheer follows, and just then, the group of boys that haven't been adjusted to the Shadows are paraded in dog chains to the middle of the crowd.

"I'm not sure, Mr. Leader, whether or not you recognize any of these boys, but they all sacrificed their morals indirectly for you and your crew. These are the ones that have earned themselves a possibility of returning to the light to live a more contributing life, to their communities, friends, families, and neighbors." The Mind recognizes all of them, many by name. He goes to them and starts telling them he's so glad they're okay, addressing them each personally. The act makes no impression on The Count or his Brethren. "You might as well stand down, boy. I'm afraid it was way too late for you years ago to be talking your way out of this fate." The mind wants to slap the Dwarf in the face; he complies instead. The large crowd splits right then; the sight of the warriors with their full headdresses on, war paint, and jewelry is more surreal than the Shadowland at night. "Did you boys think you were the first ones to tattoo and pierce your flesh?" The Count asks the nucleus of The Road Crew Mafia; they do not reply. The new arrivals are not the only spirits on this ground that are scared and confused about why the warriors are here? The Carney's had once called these men savages in the existence of the light. But, on arrival to this existence of darkness, they'd quickly formed respect for their primitive ways. "Do not fear my Brethren the arrival of the great spirit warriors. We've learned that fear of them is the truest knowledge one may gain. They've come to watch a good fight." Leonard stands beside his leader, taking off his shirt and pointing at Numb-Chuck. Numb doesn't hesitate; this human's not afraid to die or feel pain. The banger was raised religiously by his Mama, the only human he ever loved. Numb's known from a young age that God's judgment would catch up to him; this hood is happy to scrap. It could have been instant, like a bullet to the head.

The new arrival takes his shirt off; his underwear is high on a black stomach of nothing but muscle, formed through years of dedicated training in the many ways of the fight. Leonard's light flesh is not nearly as toned as his opponents; however, his skeletal structure would appear bigger if both were untrained. The Carney's cheer loud, but the leader of the warriors raises his hand and cuts it through the air, requesting silence! All that can be heard are the hooves of these apparitions closing in on the two opponents. Numb quickly shoots at Leonard, wrapping his large arms around the Carney's tree-trunk legs, attempting to take him to the ground. He's not successful; even with all that training, he just isn't strong enough to budge the good man. Leonard falls on top of him and rolls him over; he then quickly gets to his feet! "Get up, boy!" Numb does; he decides to box instead of grappling. The new arrival snaps a jab into the face of Leonard, who doesn't attempt to block it or move; the punch connects! "Get him, Chuck," Talon screams! The warriors can't wait to tamper with this one's flesh. Leonard moves in; fancy footwork allows Numb to move out of the way. Another jab snaps and lands on the Carney's face; The Road Crew Mafia cheers! Leonard drops his hands and walks towards Numb; without any dignity, the banger swings freely! Hard shot after hard shot, cuts, swells, and bloodies Leonard's face; only the new arrivals cheer! Their former pawns on dog leashes don't dare to look up from the ground. These young men have decided if given a chance; they'll live by the light. It's the voice of Joey, who holds

Stitch, that brings the exhibition to an end. "Squeeze him hard, Len!" The strike is so quick and precise. Like a rattlesnake from a coil, sinking its fangs into the leg of a muscled out stallion, Leonard charges! He wraps his being around numb, the velocity and weight taking the gangster to the ground. It's the high-pitched scream of the toughest man from Broken that puts the real fear into his fellow gangsters, who watch as their war chief's nose is bitten clean off! Leonard stands, spitting out a mouth full of blood, flesh, and cartilage. The fancy fighter is rolling around within the mass circle of flesh. His screams are not echoing in this land of Shadows but instead falling flat as if they're falling leaves on a cold fall's day.

The warriors dismount their horses in sequence. The chief walks to The Count; they shake hands and exchange some foreign phrases. The Road Crew Mafia is soon surrounded. Primitive weapons are aimed; they do not put up a fight. Soon, they're in tow, each with their hands bound on the same rope walking in a line behind the painted riders. As they struggle over the rough terrain, Numb's cries ring in their ears, as an anticipation of what waits for them at the end of this hike makes them feel nauseous. Somehow each survives as they're dragged through a bottomless black river by the strength of the horses. They're met by young natives boys and girls, who mock them in laughter before quickly running to their village to inform the tribe that a time of ritual is soon to commence. Legs that once strode across Broken Pavement immersed in the power bred by intimidation begin to fail. These gangster's hearts are entirely weakened by the sight of skull and bone, which gates this supernatural village. As the Road Crew is dragged between a long line of spirits, rocks are tossed as heavy sticks are smacked upon the evil flesh. These apparitions have no understanding or interest in the begging that runs from their lips; they only wait for the rituals of flesh to begin.

Finally, at the end of the line, bloodied and bruised, thoughts of a new life on The Island no longer existing; they come face to face with The Doc. The flesh around his jaw has been opened and hooked around his teeth. Each has been filed and is shaped highly pointy. The meat of his gums had been scaled back, giving the teeth a much longer fang-like appearance. The flesh flaps of the sliced face had individually been hooked over the shaped teeth. Even with his primitive tools, the occulted doctor had the skill of any surgeon in the light. The healing process had taken days in this dimension, and Doc had died from infection more than once. The final painting method turns facial normality into jack-o-lantern. The colors red and white create the illusion of a 3-D effect coming off of the dark skin. Appearance is not the only goal of this manipulation; Doc's unable to talk. He can only make primal screams as he has been doing while being dragged by a rope around the village. The drums commence the days of ceremony that lie ahead for these once desecrated humans. One by one, the Road Crew Mafia members that never showed empathy for the weak while thriving in the light are sat in that chair. Each has their face slit, teeth filed, and then pulled through those tiny holes. None are given any form of sedation to ease the pain. Their screams accompany the drums that pound, none with dignity as they void on themselves over and over. Once their healed and painted, the art of flesh complete, they're paraded for the rest of that day! The grey turns to red, and the sounds of the drums seem to beat from underwater. The bangers are each hung by an attachment of rope that hooks to their mouths. Each member of the Shadow-tribe, from young to old, steps up the platform and takes a cut of flesh to be eaten raw. Muted screams go on for hours in the red before what is left of these Shadows is cooked, still barely alive. The Road Crew Mafia is a feast that will be brought back through incantations spoken and honored for eternity within the Shadows.

Jessica slowly begins to awake. As she stretches her muscles, she feels as though she's appropriately positioned in bed. Upon opening her eyes, Jess's looking at a water spot on the ceiling she's seen a million times. She sits up, scanning the bed for vomit; there's none. The moment she looks at Stitch, she remembers her encounter with The Brothers. Jess feels her chest; there are fresh scratches and dry blood from the Shadowcat. The vessel remembers struggling to breathe but knowing she was going to be fine during the dark taking. Although the glowing red of their eyes and cold touch convey death, Jess had sensed peace within their presence towards her. Their movements were not aggressive. When they formed into one synergy, she'd felt as though she belonged. When her entity was left in the hallway, and The Brothers with Stitch detached and disappeared, she'd felt venerable in the Shadow-dimension. Once the Brothers had reattached to her, there was a sense that what needed to be done was finished. Jess then remembers floating past Three and big Joe. Quickly she rushes from the room, and they're at the kitchen table, drinking coffee. "I remember everything, my Count, just as Lady Dark said I would. I could feel their need for me, and it was, I mean, they were at peace when they took me in. But, this time, there was no vomit, and I woke up at the right end of the bed!" "Do you have any idea, Jess, if they accomplished what they needed to?" "I felt that when we reformed as an orb, they had. I don't how, but I do." Then, three steps close to her, wanting to appear calm, "You have said that you want this life, Jessica?" "I do, my Count." Jessica looks away, afraid he'll spot the love she feels for him. "Right now, I need you to take what you can carry quickly. I'll send for the rest to be moved after, but our Lady Dark informed me that there is danger here." Jessica nods and goes back to her bedroom; quickly, she puts on a pair of jeans and a t-shirt. After brushing her teeth, Joe helps Jess collects photos and photo albums, the urns, her gown from the Shadow Ball, and Stitch. Three's impressed by Jessica's decisiveness. Lady Dark had been very clear about the evil she'd felt that would be attached to this moment. "This is all I need from that life, my Count." "You don't require any other memories, Jess?" "All that's been good in that life is in these photos. I've lived trying to forget and forgive Three." The Count gives Joe the nod, the bodyguard speaks quietly through the door, and the guards come back in and surround Jess and the Count. They're instructed to move in sequence within the barrier of formed flesh. Moments later, they find that the elevator is out of order. Joe quickly gives instructions according to how the group will move down the stairs; guns are drawn as the situation has just opened so many more angles of vulnerability. The Lion takes the stairs with his head down; he moves stealthily, his clothing is baggy, pants hanging, as he wants to blend in. The true alpha of the Road Crew Mafia has decided that the rest of his pride is a liability. These tentacles could link him to the dark underlinings of Broken Pavement. The Killer's thirst for blood is driven by his instinct to survive as a free man. The hunter pulls the hood of his sweatshirt over his eyes when he hears the quick movement of many feet coming down the stairs. He pushes his back to the wall as he sees the solemn-looking men with guns drawn. Jessica doesn't notice his face as he gets a quick glimpse of her.

The predator quickly refocuses on the hunt in hand and continues his course up the stairs. Immediately the Lion assumes his pride has migrated as the hallway is vacant outside of the Penthouse. No guards on duty and the door is unlocked; he fears he's too late. The killer goes by the book, slowly moving within the shadows, carefully peeking around each corner. The stale marijuana smoke hovers throughout the ghetto palace like fog, heightening the hunter's senses as he isn't sure if he wandered into a trap. Soon the Lion is on the retreat, sprinting down the stairs as his eyes have just taken in an overwhelming sight of ritualistic madness. The Macomb that must have taken place within those walls reeks of a supernatural presence that this man has tried so hard to deny. But now he realizes its true power and can't help but feel as though he's been marked by something unearthly. Running may save him from those he answers to in this existence, but there's no place to hide from those that dwell in the darkness.

The ride back to Shadow Estate is quiet. While managing to keep her eyes to the window, Jessica holds Stitch, desperately trying to hide her desire. She fears her eyes will betray her. The Count's cells are activated with anticipation to what Lady Dark will tell them, hoping a vision has come to her. Upon entering the mansion, his silent prayers are answered. "You both need to come with me. I've come to learn where the darkness of Broken Pavement stems from." They follow the witch through the halls of tradition and down the stairs into the darkness. The clairvoyant can feel the supernatural that surrounds the stuffed cat. She feels its Shadow moving with them. The witch hands the newspaper article to Jessica, watching the Shadow of Stitch moving back and forth on the wall behind her. It's as though the Shadow's waiting for the cage door to be opened. "You have been in contact with this man Jessica?" "I have, but...." The Count interrupts; "You're sure, my Lady?" "I have no doubts, my Count, this is who they're calling for. This man's pound of flesh will bring balance to the scales that will restore Broken Pavement's habitat to a more natural ecosystem. The Count excuses himself from the lair of the occult. Joe is outside the door. He assures Three that he'll have an address within the hour. The Count re-enters the sacred and sits beside Jess; they listen to the witch as she instructs on how they'll proceed. "If I'm correct, my Count, The Never Sleep will be on the rails by dawn."

By the time the entire company is assembled in the great room, Joe has the Intel The Count has requested. Every member of the camp is there, including Billy Jones, who hasn't been to a season kickoff in a very long time. The traditional glasses of champagne are handed out; there's an underlying presence of excitement in the room, as always when the company is ready to begin a new campaign. "Obviously, my Brethren, you know why we're about to drink in our tradition together." The cheering begins, their leader lifts his hand to quiet them. "Please, my Brothers and Sisters, theirs been a major change in plans." The room goes quiet. There's no whispering when their leader speaks of change. "For the first time in a long time, since the only time, we'll be traveling by train." As he'd expected, there's a stench of confusion, bred by the change of destination. "Our great company is needed in a very dark place, a border-town in The Land Next Door that has been paralyzed by fear and corruption. Children can no longer play or walk the streets as they run with blood. Bullets have spawned the crimson river with no names on them. The guns being fired by those who have surrendered their souls. This campaign isn't about making money; it's about re-moving a leash of terror that has all but decimated a community of humans that deserves so much more. So, my Brethren, I'll ask you all only once; are you with me?" The Count lifts his flute of Champaign to the intense energy that rushes forward. This family has always walked in the Shadows, and they are ready to bring them forth.

Chapter 14

The Lion stares at the black and white photo of his Grandfather, the mentor he never met. His Mother had given it to him when he'd turned seven. According to her, his Grandfather had been a proud man with high ideals that lived his life by the laws of the land. The killer takes another sip; he is very intoxicated. The Lion's been drinking straight whiskey for the past four hours, trying to think his way out of the impossible situation he's faced with. Promises had been made to the corrupt power-players that run the political texture of The City. He'd sold his soul to the devil, enabling him to make vast amounts of dirty money for himself and these crooked jackals that control him. The terror he's feeling now is not what these men are capable of; it's what he's witnessed over the past days. Watching the footage of the gangbangers bones snapping while they lay paralyzed in a coma started the worrying. The Lion became paranoid that his own corrupt choices had caught up to him. Detective Smith stares at the picture of his Grandfather, Sam Smith, wishing he'd made better choices. He lays the picture face down.

Smith thinks about Talon's gruesome remains, and he shivers. The fashion of which his pupil's teeth were dug through the flesh that went around his mouth. How could his head be in such a rigid, forced-up position? As he'd walked room to room, finding each of them in such deformed states, he could feel the presence of something supernatural stalking him. The smell of rot hadn't begun, as the blood was still fresh. The Lion takes a long sip and pours another. Smith picks the picture back up and stares at the white skin of his Grandfather. Although the shade of their flesh is very contrasted, anyone could tell they're of the same blood. This hardened man starts to cry. How had he become such a bad man? At the young age of seven, his Mother, so poor, had given him this great gift, the knowledge of a legacy of a man that had been nothing short of a hero. A law legend that he could look up to and rise above his ghetto surroundings. A few months later, his Mother had been killed, stabbed to death in the elevator at Broken Pavement. The next day the young Lion had been force-fed to a system that practiced no diet of empathy to the poor and orphaned. This photo that humbles him was cared for and honored as a shrine in his breast pocket. It had helped him to wade through the muck of that vicious system, and yet here he is, alone at the end of the black rainbow, fearing what awaits him in that boiling cauldron of karma. "I'm so sorry, Grandpa." Just as this humbled killer picks up the company gun, ready to blow out the side of his head, it comes to him. The Lion quickly regains his composure as he sees the face of the young girl the men on the stairs had so evidently been protecting. As though that needed word or name hangs on one's tongue, the mind unable to recover it, the puzzle puts itself together. The riddle that Renee couldn't solve has just been answered. The Lion takes one last look at that famous lawman and puts the black and white photo in the ashtray on his desk. Soon it's no more than smoke in the air. He decides to take life from the innocent tomorrow, halting this supernatural stalking that he's felt hunting him so closely. The alpha decides to sleep; the sacrifice will be made tomorrow.

Jessica lies in the back of the motor home, staring at Stitch, who sits on a stone mantle in the back corner. The Count had given her the drink as he'd shown her the rigged bedroom on wheels. He and Joe sit in the front of which is isolated from the ad-libbed sleeping quarters. The windows are bulletproof and covered with the darkest tint, preventing light or sight from coming inside. The air is set to a flow and temperature that welcomes sleep. Jessica feels very safe as she drifts into the Darkness. The weight is gradual on her chest, growing heavy as her breathing slows. The Shadowcat grows, as does the weight. Her head snaps up. Now she's eye to eye with the red glow and rot; next is the pop. Her entity looks down upon her abnormal vessel. The expression on her face is not of panic. It picks up the Shadow of Stich and goes to The Brothers, who are turning from the corner. The giant Shadow accepts its pet. The smell of their rot is potent in this small place. The Teens spirit peacefully takes it in as she accepts the Shadow-Dwarfs icy hands. The Orb is formed; the knowledge within Jessica leads them forward. The Shadowy Orb floats unnoticed through the front yard of a house that's above the pay grade of any detective on the force, even a hero cop. The teen feels her Shadow fragment at the door; her spirit is alone in the Shadowland. This is when it becomes frightening, being vulnerable in this realm of the Shadows; caught in between the light and the Darkness.

The moment the burning current hooks into the nerves of his legs, the Lion turns into the Lamb. The weight that pushes down on his chest is that of an avalanche; his breath is taken! Smith's head snaps up to the reg glowing eyes staring down at him. The Shadow cat's energy is based upon the debt owing, and Smith's is tremendous. The claws of Darkness are even sharper and more extensive than they'd been when they'd finally dug into Carl Hester's flesh so many moons before. The corrupt Detective struggles for breath as being smothered is causing him to panic. The Lamb's head snaps up as the aggressive entity pushes down even harder. He knows his body is in the same rigid state the others had been in. Burt tries to scream; he can't, as he is overcome with the dark paralysis! It feels as though his innards are going flush through his completely stretched out mouth, and that's when he sees the three Shadows in the corner. The phantoms know Stitch has taken the unclean spirit as close to the release as possible; their movements are quick. Smith feels the cold grasp of their Shadowy hands tightly grip his ankles and wrists. Then, finally, the weight of the Shadowcat decreases, and he's able to get a slight intake of oxygen. Burt tries to move to regain his consciousness; he can't. The Lamb thinks about Renee's words, a dark existence that exists between being awake and asleep; that's when the paranormal needle enters his left wrist, as the supernatural stitching commences. The Shadow-Brothers take their time, ensuring Sam's Grandson feels each Stitch deeply. This one's ritual has been a long time coming. The bad man's conscience screams inside, ringing his cells as though they're instruments within a pinball machine! The lights bursting as bells ring, the little chrome ball being batted back and forth as the Dwarfs passionately work their dark craft. The pain of the Stitch peaks as the giant phantom attaches the Achilles Tendons to the mattress. The Shadow of Leonard is precise with his Stitch, taking his time to make sure the needle cuts through the meat of the tendon! Smith's a fighter and somehow manages to keep his jaded spirit inside his flesh. The spiritual release should have already happened. Renee's theory of a tunnel has taken shape as the glow comes through the grotesque of Hester's mouth forming on the wall! This killer's will refuses to break, somehow achieving small intakes of oxygen sporadically. Stitch digs its claws one more time before jumping from the torn chest. The Lamb feels the strength of the large one lay on him as it wraps its arms around the sides of the bed and pulls down. The Dwarfs push down on Leonard's back, but it's the final weight of Stitch that finally breaks Burt's spirit, robbing his soul of flesh and bone. Smith only has a moment to stare down at the surreal sight of his body, Stitched and smothered by the Shadows on his mattress. He's proven to be the most challenging Stitching the Shadow Brothers have ever performed; they haven't time to chase. They grab it quickly. If it weren't for the eternal fortitude of Leonard's spirit, Smith's soul would have broken free before being smuggled through the ghostly wormhole.

Theirs no grand reception for the soul of Smith. Many of these phantoms' hearts are conflicted, as Smith had shown so much promise in his youth. A man who'd only wanted to change his surroundings for the better. Without proper guidance, he'd fallen from grace through the temptations of much lesser men. The Soul of Burt Smith has been promised to Granite Grave, a jail deep in the mountains, far into the depths of chaos. It's been a very long time since the demons of Granite have received a donation. Carl Hester and his poltergeists have grown tired of the treaty. The true God's of this world and the light know the Demons are ready to bust through. Hester and his legion's energy is stronger than ever, all that is needed is a vessel, and the world of light will be submerged in the Darkness. As the Smith is put in shackles, feeling immersed in the red thick moist, The Brothers rejoin Jessica. The Orb floats back to the R.V. Soon, she awakes; her body is sore and stiff, as her spirit had been free for such a long spell. After a quick knock on the dividing glass, Jess feels the motor home move. She looks forward to a hot shower as her flesh is covered in sweat. Jess thinks about the Detective, the hero of Broken Pavement; why him, the teen asks herself? As much as he pushed her that day, she'd looked up to him. Many other policemen were casual in their protection of the poor who lived in Broken. What will happen to the Detective in the Shadowlands?

Burt feels the pressure change in his red surroundings as the Shadow-horse pulls the trailer his cage rests on; soon, he's whole as the dark grey light shines through. The sounds of the horse clicking hoofs are what he hears first; faintly, there's a conversation taking place. "Who's there;" he yells. Finally, the buggy comes to a stop. In full uniform, Marshall Sam Smith comes to the side of the adlibbed cell. For the first time, he looks into the eyes of his Grandson. The shame he feels for what he could never admit to, as when he was young having relations with someone of a different color was unacceptable, and how he'd loved her so. "Is that you, Grandpa?"

Jessica stares out the window of the train; she's never been out of The City. The teen is captivated by the significant change in vegetation as they're closed to the border into The Land Next Door. Dense forests of pines and maples have been replaced by the thick, vibrant green of the jungle. Always an honor student, Jessica had done many projects over the years about the culture, eco-systems, and most other aspects of life in the developing country that borders the Mainland. To her, the drastic change in vegetation suggests the spiked level of danger in crossing the border. Jessica is well aware of what lurks behind the green façade of the jungle; many species of poisonous snakes and spiders. To Jess, it all symbolizes her new life of danger in the Darkness. Jess stretches her muscles again. After awakening from her Dark Paralysis, she became aware of the pain suffocating her body. Although the Brothers do not mean to hurt her, the ritual takes its toll on her young body. Jessica has also been feeling a strong sense of growing dread. It's as though she's being stalked. Over and over, she stares into the green outside the window, hoping to spot an animal. But Jess knows what follows her is not of this world and is not friendly like the Brothers. Stitch sits across from her in the private car, as does her mother and Grandmother's urns. Jess feels guilty for barely thinking about either of them. Then, just as she's about to cry, there's a knock on the door. Jess quickly gets herself together and opens the door. The Count's eyes immediately calm her, center her as they have since she'd first dove into them. Jessica feels as though she's been calmly standing in the middle of a tornado. The debris of chaos spinning wildly around her; The Count keeps her grounded, safe. Jess will follow this man anywhere to any end, as she's so in love with him.

Lady Dark awakes from her dream in the back of the giant steel snake that rolls through the jungle; more has been revealed to the Clairvoyant. The Witch could see the spirit of the Detective on the other side; he was being transported somewhere very dangerous, her skin crawls at the thought of this demon land. The psychic had sensed sudden happiness in the bad man, as though he was meeting a loved one in that Darkness. The reunion was over quickly, and she had felt the sadness in the damned man; she feels his confinement and dread. A legion of demons had then raided the carriage. The small group of good

spirits had passionately fought the evil but were forced to retreat. The entity of the Detective had been freed by those that
worship the macabre of Hester.

Easing Jessica Sworn into her true life is no longer an option.
Lady Dark summons the Dwarf and sends for her Master. The
Count sees that Jessica's in pain; each time he's near her, it's
getting harder and harder for this powerful young man to turn
from his desires. "You look as though you are hurt, Jess." "I'm always sore when I wake up Three. I think it's how stiff and rigid
my body becomes during the Sleep Paralysis." Without thinking,
he puts his hands on her shoulders and begins gently massaging
them; his touch sets her being on fire. It's as though a magnetic
force pulls from her cells, her core; she lifts her head, knowing
there's no way she can hide her want. Three feels the energy,
and as much trouble as he knows this undeniable impulse could
cause, he does not turn from it; but meets it head-on. Jessica's
eyes are different; the innocence is gone, as though her soul
has aged. Neither can unlock the want that has gripped them,
so they move towards each other, their lips ready to touch, and
then comes the knock at the door. The Count snaps back to reality quickly, giving her a look to suggest he'd forgotten his place
for a moment, and then he opens the door. "What are you doing
here?" Jessica smiles at the handsome Dwarf. "The Lady needs
you now, My Count; it's of the most urgent of business. I've been
instructed to have that talk with Jess now while you go to her."
Three feels bad for Jessica as he tells her goodbye and quickly
heads to the caboose. Jessica loses her balance, almost fainting
when she looks at the face of the muscled-out short man.

The Count rushes through each car, ignoring his Brethren,
who smile and call for his attention. These loyal humans prepare
themselves for the dark unknown they're entering into; seeing
the urgency on their leader's face increases, they're anticipation.
The foreign look of sadness and fright he sees on The Lady's face
startles him; she's always been confident. "We need to find out if
the body or remains of Smith are still at his house, My Count."
"Why?" "I don't have time to explain my Count, but something

has happened in the Darkness, a change of the balance that has kept certain evils at bay. Please, there's no time to discuss why's in this moment;" her voice is shaky, marinated in panic. The Count steps out of the car; he summons Joe over the trains P.A. The bodyguard is always ready to serve, goes to the caboose. "We need to know if Smith's body is still in the house, Joe." "It will take a few minutes, My Count, as my associates left the premises hours ago." "As you will," and the call is made.Jessica is speechless as she stares at Jessie; it's as though she's looking into a mirror. As he tells her that he's her Uncle, her Mother's twin brother; It's confirmed many miles away that the body of Detective Burt Smith is gone, and there are no signs of blood spilled.

To be continued...

www.ingramcontent.com/pod-product-compliance
Lightning Source LLC
Chambersburg PA
CBHW051944170626
46808CB00007B/2473